*Look what people are saying about*
*Suzanne Forster...*

"Suzanne Forster mixes heat with humor in a
tale filled with plenty of heart."
—*The Best Reviews* on *Brief Encounters*

"*Brief Encounters* by Suzanne Forster dishes
up a sexy, hilarious romantic romp."
—*Romantic Times BOOKclub*

"With Suzanne Forster, Harlequin found a very
talented author to launch their sexy books
and if you are looking for a sexual adventure
and something different to all the new erotic
romance titles, then *Tease* should go
at the top of your reading list."
—*A Romance Review*

"With...*Come Midnight*, the extremely
talented Suzanne Forster delivers one of
the sexiest psychological suspense
tales to come along in years."
—*Romantic Times BOOKclub*

# Blaze™

Dear Reader,

Is there anything better than a darkly mysterious man?
How about shadowing that man, staking him out and
all but kidnapping him to use for your own private
purposes, such as getting into a decadent, members-only
gentlemen's club? And then, when things get desperate
and he starts to question your cover as one of the club's
hostesses, how about convincing him that you are as
outrageously sensual as you pretend to be?

Those are just some of the feats that Ally Danner, my
heroine in *Decadent,* must accomplish. Fortunately, Ally
is highly motivated. She has a sister she believes is being
held in the club against her will, and Ally feels directly
responsible for her sibling's situation. After all, it was
Ally who was the bad girl once upon a time, and now her
baby sister seems to be following in her footsteps.

I could go on and on about *Decadent,* but that would
spoil the fun—and I did have such delicious fun writing
about the adventures of Ally and her darkly mysterious
hero, Sam Sinclair, a wickedly sexy adversary, if ever there
was one.

In addition to Sam and Ally, you'll meet some other
characters in the upcoming pages, including a couple of
ghosts who haunt the elegant old mansion that houses
the gentlemen's club. A centuries-old secret ties these
star-crossed lovers into the present-day story, and I hope
you'll be as intrigued by their shadowy presence as I was.

Enjoy the decadent fun!

*Suzanne Forster*

# SUZANNE FORSTER

## *Decadent*

HARLEQUIN®

TORONTO • NEW YORK • LONDON
AMSTERDAM • PARIS • SYDNEY • HAMBURG
STOCKHOLM • ATHENS • TOKYO • MILAN • MADRID
PRAGUE • WARSAW • BUDAPEST • AUCKLAND

ISBN-13: 978-0-373-79292-4
ISBN-10:    0-373-79292-1

DECADENT

## ABOUT THE AUTHOR

*New York Times* bestselling author Suzanne Forster has written over thirty novels and has been the recipient of countless awards. Her many television and print appearances include NBC's *Extra,* CBS's Emmy Award-winning "Special Report" on Channel 23, the *L.A. Times,* the *Philadelphia Inquirer* and *Redbook.* Suzanne has a master's degree in writing popular fiction, and lives in Newport Beach, California, where she is at work on her next novel.

Suzanne can be contacted at www.suzanneforster.com.

## Books by Suzanne Forster
HARLEQUIN BLAZE
101—BRIEF ENCOUNTERS
125—UNFINISHED BUSINESS

Don't miss any of our special offers. Write to us at the following address for information on our newest releases.

Harlequin Reader Service
U.S.: 3010 Walden Ave., P.O. Box 1325, Buffalo, NY 14269
Canadian: P.O. Box 609, Fort Erie, Ont. L2A 5X3

This one is for the wonderful fans and friends who have done me the honor of becoming members of my Yahoo Group. You guys are the best! Thank you for supporting me through even the toughest times, and know that I will never forget your outpouring of love and sympathy when I lost my mother. It meant more than I can possibly express.

# 1

*RUN, ALLY! Stop staring at him and run. He's evil. Don't let him touch you!*

But as the forbidding figure moved through the mist toward her, Ally couldn't run. His physical domination of everything surrounding him in the ancient cemetery seemed to hold her like a net.

She'd heard the tales about the Wolverton legend and the ghost that haunted The Willows, an elegant old mansion. According to folklore, the estate had been stolen from the Wolvertons nearly a hundred years ago, and Micha Wolverton had been killed trying to reclaim it. His dying vow had been to be reunited with the spirit of his beloved wife, who'd taken her life for reasons no one would speak of, except in whispers. But Ally had never put much stock in the fantasy. She didn't believe in ghosts.

Until now—

She didn't understand what was happening. The figure had just materialized out of the mist, his body solidifying right before her eyes.

His face was familiar...so familiar. She stepped back as he approached.

"Don't be afraid," he murmured. His voice wasn't what she had expected. It didn't sound as if it were coming *from beyond the grave. It was deep and sensual. Commanding.*

*"Who are you?" she managed.*

*"You should know. You summoned me."*

*"No, I didn't." Two minutes ago, she'd been crouching behind a moss-covered crypt, spying on the mansion that had once been The Willows, but was now Club Casablanca. And then this—*

*If he was Micha, he might be angry that she was trespassing on his property. "I'll go," she said. "I won't come back. I promise."*

*"You're not going anywhere."*

*Words snagged in her throat. "Wh-why not? What do you want?"*

*"If I wanted something, Ally, I'd take it. This is about need."*

*She tried to back away, but her feet were useless. "And you need something from me?"*

*"Good guess." His tone burned with irony. "I need lips, soft and surrendered, a body limp with desire."*

*"My lips, my bod—?"*

*"Only yours."*

*"Why? Why me?" This couldn't be Micha. He had wanted only one woman, Rose, and he had died trying to return to her.*

*"Because you want that, too," he said.*

*Wanted what? A ghost of her own? She'd always found the legend impossibly romantic. How could he have known that? How could he know anything about her? Besides, she'd sworn off inappropriate men, and what could be more inappropriate than a ghost? She shook her head again, still not willing to admit the truth. But her pounding heart wouldn't play along. The mere thought of his kiss, his touch, terrified her. This wildness, it was fear, wasn't it?*

When his fingertips touched her cheek, she flinched, expecting his flesh to be cold, lifeless. It was anything but that. His skin was smooth and hot, gentle, yet demanding. And while his dark brown eyes were filled with mystery and wonder, there was a sensitivity about them that threatened to disarm her if she gazed too deeply.

"These lips are mine," he said. In truth, it was just that. She couldn't stop him...and didn't want to.

"I've come back to claim them," he whispered as his mouth descended onto hers and his powerful arms encircled her body.

If he were to touch her breasts, he would know how hard her heart was beating. She realized that as the promised kiss became a reality. His mouth ravished hers. Not gentle or tender, he kissed her with dark, whispering force, his lips moving over hers, claiming, then taking, brushing and licking, softening her mouth until it could do nothing but respond to him.

With a sigh of resignation, she surrendered to his advances. His hand stole up her body and stroked her breasts. Beneath her clothing, her nipples responded, tightening as he brushed them with his thumbs.

The tingling she felt was quick and sharp, creating a surge of desire.

Was he going to make love to her? She didn't know. As his kiss deepened, she gave way to the hypnotic power of his spellbinding caresses. Her entire body was thrumming and buzzing. Alive and free again.

Buzzing and buzzing...like...an insect?

It filled her senses, growing louder.

*What was that sound? A bumblebee?*

Ally's eyes blinked open, and she smacked her arm with an open palm. Not a bumblebee, a mosquito—a bloodsucking mosquito! She must have dozed off. The seventy-plus hours without sleep had caught up with her. She would never have fallen asleep in a cemetery unless she was exhausted. No one would.

She took a quick look around to make sure she hadn't been spotted by any of the club's security guards. She didn't see anyone headed her way, nor were there any tall, dark figures fleeing the scene.

A dream. Of course, what else? The question she ought to be asking was why she was slinking around an abandoned graveyard on a cloud-swollen, moonless night. It wasn't the place most women went to look for a man, especially considering why she needed one, but Ally had no choice. Some things had to be done—and in her twenty-eight years of life, little had been more crucial than her mission tonight.

Her younger sister, Victoria, was being held captive in the mansion not a hundred yards from where Ally now hid. Originally, Club Casablanca had been the country estate of the Wolvertons, a genteel farming family. They had it built about sixty miles north of New Orleans where the water table allowed for basements, tunnels and other subterranean secrets. Once a graceful Georgian plantation house, it now reminded Ally of Count Dracula's castle. In some dark, terrifying way it was even more beautiful than before with its turrets and arches, especially at night. But it was also a den of depravity disguised as an exclusive, private gentleman's club.

Ally brushed the dirt and leaves from her black suit, a

Chanel look-alike with a skirt she'd shortened herself. She planned to say she was job hunting if the guards should spot her. In case the short skirt didn't convince them she'd make a red-hot hostess, she'd worn a low-cut cream silk camisole under her jacket. Thank God it was spring or else she would have frozen in so little clothing.

She'd chosen the graveyard for her stakeout, knowing the club's security cameras didn't survey this area. Actually, there was a lot she knew about Club Casablanca from personal experience, all of which she'd tried very hard to forget. Her sister's disappearance, however, had made that impossible. Just three days ago, Vix had sent a bizarre e-mail, implying that she was being held here against her will. She didn't say much more than that, but sirens had gone off in Ally's head.

Ally had worked at the club as a hostess in her early twenties, and had foolishly let herself be drawn into a destructive relationship with its owner, Jason Aragon. She'd barely escaped Aragon with her life. This e-mail suggested that she may not have escaped him after all. She had little doubt that he was trying to lure her back, using her sister as bait—and her sister was much too young, naive and rebellious to resist the pressures and temptations of such a place.

Just as Ally had been.

She tugged at her skirt, but the hem kept crawling up her thighs and making her feel naked—a nagging reminder of the mistakes of her past. Perhaps her fall had been preordained, given her childhood. Overprotected from the cradle, her life choices rigidly controlled, supposedly for her own good, but she'd felt confined, suffocated. It hadn't been quite so bad for Vix, but almost.

Ally still went to great effort to keep everything about her past secret, mostly to protect her aristocratic family from any more embarrassment. She and her sister were heirs to a throne that no longer existed. Their mother had been a sitting queen, strange as that seemed in today's world, and her arranged marriage to their father had been a happy one until the royal couple had been deposed and exiled from the small European monarchy where Ally's mother's family had reigned for over a century.

Ally had been thirteen when the family had fled to London. Soon after, she had been sent to America to an exclusive all-girls' boarding school, but it turned out not to be the move toward independence Ally had hoped for. The bodyguards her family had hired to protect her made her already lonely and isolated life seem like a prison. The last straw had come when she'd graduated Alderwood Academy and learned that her parents were intent on marrying her off to a man she'd never met, a wealthy German industrialist.

That had been when Ally had discovered she had a will of her own—and a wild streak, which Jason Aragon had been happy to help her explore.

A sigh of regret escaped her. There really hadn't been any other men in her life except a couple of fleeting summer romances with prep school boys. But she'd made up for it with Jason. She'd gone wild, reveling in everything that had been forbidden to someone of her background, and then some. It had been a temporary lapse, but bad enough that she'd disgraced the family name. Now Vix seemed ready to take up where Ally had left off. And Ally felt responsible.

Her sister had lived with their parents in London until

four years ago when they'd decided to send Vix to Alder-wood, too. The school had a sterling reputation, and Ally had begged her parents to let Vix attend, promising to keep a close eye on her. Ally had seen it as a chance to redeem herself in her family's eyes and to renew the bond with her younger sister.

Vix had lived at Alderwood, spending weekends and holidays with Ally in her Georgetown apartment in Washington, D.C. If anything, Ally had been overly strict. However, a few months ago she'd snagged a promotion that had made it impossible to keep such close tabs on her sister. About that same time Vix had begun missing classes and staying out after curfew with her latest boyfriend, whom Ally didn't approve of.

A revving car engine jerked Ally out of her reflections. She peeked around the crypt, reminding herself to keep an eye on the club's entrance. She'd already used up three days of her personal leave, and she only had a week in total. Her new position as director of development at the Smithsonian involved finding deep-pocketed donors for the institute's conservation projects. The job was high-profile, as well as high-pressure, but luckily, she'd been there several years and had taken off so little time that her boss approved her request for leave without question. Ally had been on a flight out of Dulles within hours of receiving Vix's e-mail.

She'd debated calling the New Orleans police, not sure they would investigate based on one vague e-mail. In any case, Vix's e-mail had asked her not to involve the police. So Ally was on her own.

Her first task had been to set up a surveillance plan. Now she needed to get inside the club. For that she had to have an escort, a member of the male-only kind. Women were welcome, only as guests of members or as club employees. That was the tricky part. If she approached the wrong man in the wrong way, both she and Vix might be put in grave danger.

She continued to peer around the crypt watching cars pull into the club's crescent driveway. She was looking for one in particular, and hoped she hadn't missed the mystery man who drove the sleek black Porsche Targa.

Ally glanced at the luminous dial of her watch— 8:58 p.m. If he kept to his routine, he should arrive in the next two or three minutes. When it came to punctuality, he was as reliable as a Swiss timepiece. Still, over the course of the last seventy-two hours—long, exhausting hours in which she had attempted to stalk his every move—she'd become convinced that he wasn't just another member of the club. He was up to something clandestine.

She'd singled him out the very first night, after watching dozens of men arrive and leave. It didn't hurt that he was tall and ruggedly built. She'd had a gut feeling about him, and that was as precisely as she could define it for now. That was when she'd begun tailing him as he went through his daily routine, which was anything but routine.

Twice a day he'd left his hotel to take walks, and his destination was always a different pay phone where he would place a brief call. Obviously he didn't feel safe using the phone in his room. Who was he calling? He could be a private investigator, an undercover cop or an FBI or CIA agent, calling in from the field. He might even be a master thief planning a heist of the club's valuable art collection.

*How would a master thief make love to a woman?*

The thought came from out of nowhere. She tried to force her attention back to the cars pulling into the club, but it refused to stay there. Apparently it still craved the thrill a man like that could give her, pleasure at any cost. That alone should have appalled her. One silly second of fantasizing about a gorgeous man's hands wandering like a thief's over her body, stealing her will to resist—*to deny him anything*—and she was on the brink of losing it.

Pathetic. She had clearly gone way too long without sex. *But Ally Danner didn't do those things anymore. She didn't lust after inappropriate men, and this guy couldn't be more inappropriate.* Cop? FBI or CIA agent? Thief? Probably he was a straying husband. The possibilities were endless, and she had to know exactly what he was up to before she made her move.

She crouched even lower, moving clear of the crypt for a better view. *He's clever and dangerous,* she told herself. *Don't forget that. And you—*

*You haven't had sex in a* very *long time.*

Ignoring the hot little tingle in her gut, she moved on. Last night he'd left the club at eleven, and she'd followed him in her rental car to the oak forest behind the club. She'd lost him though when she had to turn off the car lights to avoid being spotted. He and his black Targa had melted into the moss-draped trees, and she'd held back, fearing a trap. Instead she'd returned the next day, and searched the area on foot.

She'd been ready to give up when she came across a path of beaten-down underbrush leading to an abandoned car in a clearing. She'd searched the interior and found nothing. When she opened the hood though, she'd discovered the car had no engine. The space was filled with surveillance equipment that looked designed to pick up long-range audio signals, possibly through the spiral rod that emerged from the opening where the radio antenna should have been.

At that point she'd made a decision. If he were trying to infiltrate the club, that might mean they could help each other. She needed an escort—and she had insider information that could be useful to him. If he were acting privately, she had a better chance of striking a bargain with him than if he were law enforcement, but she had to know which it was, and that brought her to the riskiest part of her plan. Unmasking him.

Strange as it seemed, the only thing stopping her now was his face. The first time she'd seen him, she'd had a nagging feeling of déjà vu. And then, tonight, this dream. Something about the ghost had brought about that same feeling. Not that they were the same man, necessarily, but something.

She was beginning to wonder if her erotic dream had been a warning from her subconscious. Was it signaling that she had something to fear from this man, that he was a danger to her?

She knew what went on inside the mansion walls. The upper floors resembled a lavish Monte Carlo casino. The subterranean level catered to darker, more exotic tastes, to put it mildly. It was accessible only to platinum key members, hand-selected by Jason, who were willing to undergo a deep background search, and of course, to pay a small fortune in membership fees.

Was her man one of those? Did he have such exotic tastes? Maybe that was what the dream had been trying to tell her?

*If I wanted something, Ally, I'd take it. This is about need.*

Another growling car engine brought her back to the present. She glanced up to see a Targa pull into the driveway. A tuxedo-clad man exited the front door of the club and rushed down the white marble steps, ready as the car roared to a halt. Ally didn't recognize the valet from her time with Jason, but she knew his résumé would have included thug, bouncer, and perhaps even worse, right along with valet. Most likely he was armed.

Ally watched as her man emerged from the car. She was about a hundred yards away, not close enough to see him clearly, but she knew his features, detail for detail. He was six feet plus with thick, dark blond hair and skin so tawny she was reminded of windswept deserts. Even his eyebrows had a dust-covered look that she found annoyingly irresistible. As the valet drove off in the Targa, her subject snapped his black leather jacket into place, and then casually adjusted his tan slacks, as if the drive had somehow left him a bit out of order down there. It wasn't a crude movement. If anything, it was gracefully sensual in a male sort of way.

And it sent Ally's stomach spinning, along with her imagination.

She didn't even know this man. Why was she reacting to him this way? Unless she did know him.

He checked his watch, possibly to disguise the fact that he was subtly scanning his surroundings as he made his way up the steps. If he held to his routine, he would be inside for at least two hours, maybe longer, and that was more than enough time for her to carry out her plan.

Then he stopped midway—and Ally's heart stopped with him.

He turned and looked straight at her.

He couldn't see her in the dark, could he? She was down on her knees. Fear set fire to her lungs as he strode back down the steps. She inched back toward the stone, certain that she'd been spotted. There was nothing she could do now but hug the ground and beseech the heavens. If she moved, she would give herself away.

She heard footsteps coming her way, and felt the ground shake.

"I'd heard the club was haunted," said a faintly sardonic male voice. "Instead of a ghost, I find a beautiful woman crawling around the graveyard. Obviously you've lost a contact lens, right?"

Ally felt something inside her go cold as she looked up at him, and it wasn't just fear that silenced her. It was the odd sense of recognition she'd experienced before. How strange that he'd mentioned the club was haunted, and just now for a second she'd thought she was staring into the eyes of a ghost. Her ghost. The one she'd dreamed about. Too weird. It was fatigue, stress.

"You can't speak?" he teased.

*She* never got a chance to try. The guards were shouting at him from the entrance.

"Need any help?" one of them called out.

"Did you find anything over there?" the other yelled.

"Looks like I caught a little cemetery mouse," the man told them, still gazing down at Ally so intently she didn't dare move. She'd gripped a handful of leaves, and she couldn't let go of them. They were crumpled in her fists.

*What was he going to do?*

"It's probably a freaking rat," the first guard said. "I'll take it out."

Ally peeked around the man and saw the guard draw his gun. He started toward them, and she let out a tiny squeak of alarm. She was going to be shot.

"Too late," the man said. "I scared it away."

His gaze commanded Ally to get back behind the stone, yet she couldn't move. The guard broke into a jog, obviously relishing the chance at some action even if it was a measly rodent. He was just ten feet away when the man wheeled around and walked straight at him, stopping him in his tracks. The man's voice was hard enough to dent steel.

"Put it away!" he ordered the guard.

"Absolutely, sir, sorry!"

While the guard struggled to holster his weapon, Ally crept back behind the crypt. She nearly collapsed with relief as the two men returned to the club. Close call. Much too close. She had no idea why the man had given her a break. This well might be her only chance to escape. Her car was parked on the other side of the cemetery, far away from the club's entrance, and she wasn't sure she could make it.

Sheer nerve and adrenaline drove Ally to her feet. When she looked back at the mansion, the man had just entered the club and the valet was busy helping guests out of a limo. Both guards were engaged in conversation, probably about the rat that got away, which meant Ally still had time. All she had to do was find her way through the graveyard.

She hadn't gone far before it became apparent that she was trying to outrun a storm. The tumultuous night sky promised to become violent. She moved faster. He'd diverted the guards when he could just as easily have turned her in. What did that mean? She could only speculate. Was he playing with her? Did he have some plan to trap her?

She would have to take that chance. Her gut was still telling her this was her man. She'd already determined that he wasn't an established member of the club, with an allegiance to Aragon. The valets were trained to recognize members on sight, and none of them had recognized this man. They'd each given him a claim ticket when they parked his car. Even more significant, he was spying on the club himself.

With luck, she could be back in New Orleans in less than an hour. And with a little more luck—and a key card obtained from a surprisingly helpful young hotel maid— she would be searching the man's hotel room. If her search proved what she already suspected—that he was trying to infiltrate the club's inner circle—then she could be of help to him. More than anything she needed this stranger to be the *right* man, and so far it looked good. He had already accomplished what she could not accomplish alone. He had entered the belly of the beast.

As she drove through the night, she went over what she knew about him, gleaned from the hotel staff where he was staying. He was said to be a corporate raider of some sort. Supposedly wealthy. He loved high-stakes gambling. He didn't have a woman with him. And his name was Sam.

# 2

SAM SINCLAIR had a woman on his mind. Too bad it didn't happen to be the attractive security guard creature in the form-fitting uniform busily frisking him. Her happy little fingers delved inside his jacket, playing patty-cake with his pecs and abs. Roaming upward, she smiled at him as if this were all in a day's work for her, which was pretty accurate from what he'd observed.

"You have thirty minutes to stop that," he said as she dropped to her knees and proceeded to pat down his privates. Nothing very private about the way she fondled him, although it was certainly thorough.

So, with all this attention coming his way, why was he fantasizing about his dark-haired stalker out there in the graveyard? If he'd had his choice of a woman down on her knees in front of him, it would have been her.

He could still see her big bright eyes peering up at him in dismay. She'd looked a little dazed and disheveled, her mouth open in surprise. Call him a perverse bastard, but that had struck him as *incredibly* sexy. Even now, the image of her parted lips elicited a warm, full sensation in his groin, and he warned himself to be careful. He wasn't carrying a weapon, but the security guard might soon have reason to think so. He'd be as primed and ready as the gun he kept concealed in his car. At least *it* had a safety switch. Somehow his dark-haired stalker had unlocked his.

From the moment he'd spotted her following him three days ago, she'd had his attention beyond the obvious professional concerns. It was personal, although he hadn't yet figured out why. Maybe he liked the idea of being tailed by a beautiful amateur. Or maybe he just hadn't had enough tail lately. How long *had* it been?

"You're good," the security guard said, glancing up at him from her kneeling position at his crotch. "To go," she added with a wink.

"Sorry to hear that."

He was now free to enter the club itself. Provisional members were subjected to full body pat-downs until they'd been approved. No one seemed to object especially since the pat-down crew were all women. But Sam knew it was a serious search. If he'd resisted, she would have called for backup, and he would have been escorted out by several hulks in tuxedoes.

The anteroom, where he'd been detained, was octagonal, gilded in gold and adorned with erotic murals. Sam smiled inwardly at the thought of Micha Wolverton's reaction to the orgiastic scenes. Legend had it that Micha roamed the grounds of the club, trying to reclaim the mansion—and the wife—that had been stolen from him a century ago by a forebear of Jason Aragon's. Aragon took great care to keep that information under wraps.

A set of ornately carved mahogany double doors opened into the main foyer. The attractive pat-down artist slipped around Sam and placed her hands on the gleaming brass doorknobs. "Enjoy," she said.

"How could I not?"

"Ah, Mr. Sinclair, how nice to see you again."

Angelic Dupree, the club's manager, greeted him as the doors opened to a huge, breathtakingly beautiful foyer. The slight, sweet-faced young woman, gowned in chiffon and feathers, ran the club herself, and apparently with dainty fists made of iron. She'd been the manager when Aragon had taken ownership, and he'd kept her on. She oversaw everything from the finances to the mint julep toothpicks used at the bar.

Sam took her extended hand. As was the custom at the club, he bent and kissed it. He thought he heard her purr, knowing it was simply for effect. Angelic might look like a wide-eyed kitten, but a man would be wise not to casually turn his back on her.

Her long, flowing white slip of a dress complemented the caramel latté tones of her skin. No one knew much about her background, except that she'd been raised in poverty in a shanty not far from where they now stood. Sam didn't know the details of the history between Angelic and Aragon. He imagined it would make one hell of a story. He wondered what price she'd paid for Aragon's *kindness*. Aragon did nothing for free.

"Thank you for the warm reception," Sam replied.

"Our pleasure. Mr. Aragon will be with you soon. He's looking forward to meeting with you tonight. In the meantime, please accept our hospitality. I believe we have your favorite drink on the way. Beefeater on the rocks with a twist, isn't it?"

Sam smiled, and she inclined her head slightly, her golden eyes never leaving him. "I'm told you've been asking about our ghosts."

Interesting that it had gotten back to her so quickly.

Sam made a mental note of that. Evidently all roads here led back to Angelic.

He decided to come clean. "On a tour of the club, one of your hostesses warned me about the master bedroom in the east wing. She said it was original to the house, and the woman who died there haunts the room."

Angelic smiled. "Not just the room. The White Rose haunts the entire house, though that's where she does most of her mischief. Her real name was Rose Wolverton. Those who've glimpsed her say she wears the same sheer white nightgown she wore when she took her own life in that east wing bedroom."

"Took her life?" Sam probably knew the story better than Angelic did, but he had reasons for keeping that to himself. He also had reasons for wanting to know how the White Rose supposedly haunted the place now. Her "mischief" could prove to be an excellent cover for some of his plans.

"It's really quite sad," Angelic said, though the sparkle in her eyes revealed she enjoyed the scandalous gossip. "Rose and her husband, Micha, had two children. She wanted more, and for some reason he didn't. They say she was unstable and so outraged at his refusal that she allowed herself to be seduced by his business partner, hoping to become pregnant anyway."

She raised her lovely eyebrows, as if to suggest that the good part was coming. "Only Rose didn't get pregnant, and the partner used blackmail to force her into more sex. She became extremely distraught. It was Micha she loved, and she knew it would kill him if he ever found out, so she killed herself—in quite a horrible way."

Sam didn't need Angelic to tell him how horrible it

was—or what had happened after that. Rose had stabbed herself in the chest—in the heart, to be exact. Micha had found her that way, and had never recovered. Despondent, he drank and gambled everything away, eventually losing even the house and the business to his partner in a poker game.

"His business partner sounds like the real villain," Sam said, curious how Angelic would react.

Her eyes gleamed. "Yes, Jake Colby. He actually told Micha about the sex, gloated over it. Micha tried to kill him and was sentenced to ten years in prison. It was terribly sad. The children were sent away to live with an aunt."

Sam nodded. Angelic was well-informed, but apparently even she didn't know that Colby's only daughter had married an Aragon, and that was how The Willows had come to be a gentlemen's club, decadent and corrupt to the core.

Angelic's sigh sounded sincere. "That's why Rose weeps. I've never heard her, but people say you can, if you listen. And you can always tell when she's near by the rose-scented perfume she wears."

"And the icy cold breeze?"

"Yes, how did you know?"

Sam shrugged. "Don't all ghosts usher in icy cold breezes?"

"This one also slams doors on fingers and drops light fixtures on your head. Rose isn't a happy ghost. And neither is Micha. People say the pounding is him, trying to get back in the house to her."

The way Sam had heard it, Micha had tried to break into The Willows when he was released from prison, and he was shot by Colby in the graveyard, which was just under the bedroom window where Rose looked out.

"I'll stay clear of the east wing," Sam promised.

"Please." Angelic glanced at her jeweled watch. "And now, if you'll excuse me, I'll leave you to await Mr. Aragon."

The sparkle was gone from her voice as she said goodbye and glided off in the general direction of the club's ground-floor lounge, chiffon fluttering behind her.

Sam would almost have thought she believed the ghost stories. He hoped she did. The more people who believed them the better, given what he had in mind. Tonight though, his primary concern was making Jason Aragon believe that he was the perfect candidate for membership.

Sam had made several visits to the club in the two weeks he'd been in New Orleans. He'd known there would be extensive background checks that included his finances and anything else they could dig up, but "Sam Sinclair" looked good on paper. Of course, it was all fake documentation, a cover, but an impenetrable one. The people he worked for didn't miss a trick. His real surname wasn't Sinclair.

He was well-prepared. Nonetheless, the wild card in the deck was Aragon himself. It didn't matter how well-prepared you were. If you didn't pass muster with Aragon personally, you weren't invited into the inner circle.

Tonight he would meet the man, face-to-face. Meanwhile, he would do a little harmless browsing. Gleaming black-and-white marble stretched before him as he entered the seemingly endless foyer. Some fifty feet away, twin staircases, dressed in royal blue carpeting with elaborate gold borders, curved like a woman's hips to the second floor. Between them stood an ornate wrought-iron cage that served as an elevator.

The female operator was the sole exception to the

smiling hostesses and security guards. She didn't look as if she'd so much as *consider* cracking a smile. This one was all business, and that made sense for she was the first line of defense on the journey to the restricted lower level.

As he considered his opulent surroundings, a woman in black drifted by on the arm of a member. Her revealing sheath and sequined mask made Sam think of his very determined shadow. He wondered if he'd scared her off, or if she was still outside, perhaps watching from her rental car. Amazing that the club's security system hadn't spotted her yet. Maybe Aragon needed to be wised-up. His legendary Ziploc perimeter was being threatened by a baby Femme Nikita in black with the sexiest red valentine of a mouth Sam had ever seen.

Immediately to Sam's left was the portal leading to the Gentlemen's Lounge, a dark, intimate setting housing a thirty-foot mahogany bar and a sumptuous buffet. There was also a five-star restaurant for serious gourmands. Sam had no time for food at the moment. He strolled to his right and entered the Grand Salon, a ballroom that featured several of the club's unique perks.

The first thing that caught his eye, as it did every time he came here, were the two life-size Victorian-style bird-cages hanging from the ceiling. Inside each gold-plated cage sat a feathery clad woman, perched on a swing. He knew from experience that if he came within three feet of either cage, the captive inside would softly and seductively promise him *anything* if he would only release her. The offers were tempting but, unfortunately, only fully pledged members were allowed keys to the locked doors. With a little luck, he'd have one of those keys in his pocket tonight.

Naturally, he'd envisioned a sneaky little brunette cooing to him from one of the cages. Not a bad idea, actually. Lock her up until she sang. He'd find out what she was up to and determine the level of threat she posed. How would she look in feathers? Better yet, out of feathers. Would she crack if he plucked them one by one, then tickled her slowly and mercilessly with her own plumage? Would she crack if he teased her entire body with the tip of his tongue, starting with her naked mouth? God, how he would love to indulge in those lips of hers at his leisure.

*Hell, do you want to find out what she's up to, or do you just want to see the woman crack?*

The breath he released was as heated as his thoughts. He could feel blood rising feverishly to the surface of his skin. The tension in his groin was rising, too. Interesting that a woman could infect his thoughts that way, like a virus. That hadn't happened in a long time.

The hostess who appeared with his drink was a welcome distraction. She was costumed like a thirties movie siren, as were all the other hostesses. Greta Garbo had nothing on any of them. Their shoulder pads were ample, their necklines deep and their cloche hats had sheer black veils that covered their faces. It wasn't complete anonymity, but it was close. Silky, seamed stockings and platform heels finished off the look.

The overall effect was highly erotic, but Sam sure as hell wasn't going where his mind wanted to. God, no, he wasn't going there. His fantasy stalker had made enough costume changes for one night.

"Can I get you anything else?" the hostess asked as Sam took his drink.

He shook his head, wanting her gone, along with the image of the woman she'd stirred. "Nothing, thanks."

She smiled, slyly taking in his physique with her lingering gaze. "If you need anything later…anything at all, just ask."

"I'll keep that in mind," he said.

"Mr. Sinclair." Sam turned to face the baritone voice that had just spoken his name, Jason Aragon. Angelic Dupree was at his side.

"We are so happy to see you," Aragon said, extending his hand.

Jason Aragon was every bit as impressive as his club. At six feet plus and solidly built, he didn't just stand in a space, he *occupied* it. Even dressed as he was tonight in a tux trimmed with black satin, he seemed formidable. His short-cropped hair was as white as snow and his eyes as shockingly blue as an Icelandic lake in winter. He was not the sort of man you messed with and lived to tell about it.

A hostess appeared magically to relieve Sam of his untouched drink.

"Thank you for the invitation," Sam said as he clasped Aragon's hand. His grip was firm but not forceful. *Controlled* was the word that came to Sam's mind. Even Aragon's gaze fell into that category. It was focused, yet friendly. Sam knew he was being sized up.

"Join me," Aragon said, indicating the interior of the spacious room. The two of them walked side by side, Angelic falling behind.

"The club seems quiet tonight. Is that normal?" Sam had been told that certain platinum key members, otherwise known as the inner circle, met in great secrecy one night a week to discuss world economic events. He imagined they were probably being briefed on the latest international financial data, undoubtedly picking up insider tips, as well as discussing the imminent rise and fall of various world markets. Sam's interest was limited to how Aragon made it possible for them to hide vast sums of money.

"As I'm sure you now realize," Aragon said, "most of our clientele are men of some stature, and without being too simplistic, such men have problems to solve. The ability to concisely solve a complex problem is the first trait of a superior mind. Wouldn't you agree?"

"One of them, certainly," Sam said.

"And what's another?" Aragon asked.

The unexpected question made Sam wonder if this was a pop quiz. He should have brushed up on Nietzsche's Superman theory. "In my line of work, solving problems is essential," he said, "but preventing them is better. I'd say foresight is the most important trait of a superior mind."

Aragon smiled, clearly pleased with Sam's answer. He held his hand out and Angelic placed a platinum key in his palm. "I'm afraid we don't stand on ceremony here," he said. "Once a person has been approved for membership, it's simply a matter of giving him his key. You now have free and unrestricted access to all levels of the club."

Aragon flourished the glimmering bauble before he offered it to Sam.

"Honored," Sam said, accepting the key. It was ceremonial more than anything else, but the symbolism was obvious. Aragon giveth, and Aragon can taketh away.

"I know how selective you are," Sam said, "and how *discreet*." He glanced at Angelic, and Aragon picked up on the signal instantly.

"That will be all," Aragon told her.

With a slight nod of her head, Angelic turned and left. Sam wondered again if her docility was an act. If so, she was good. Aragon seemed to be watching her, too, though without a hint of lust in his expression. Maybe they weren't mixing pleasure with business?

"I'd suggest a glass of champagne to celebrate," Aragon said, "but I have a plane to catch tomorrow, and some pressing things to finish up before I go."

Aragon was leaving? Now or never, Sam realized. "I have it on good authority that your contacts in international financial spheres are vast," he said. "If that's true, there's a certain problem you may be able to advise me on."

Aragon's ice blue eyes warmed a little. "Would that be the four hundred and seven million dollars you funneled from Tricon Electronics—or the one hundred and nine million from Laurent Enterprises?"

"Both." Sam nodded. "And my compliments to your people."

"There's very little we *don't* know about you," Aragon said. "Otherwise, you wouldn't be here."

The two traded glances. Somewhere in the exchange a silent agreement was made that this conversation would continue in the near future.

"I have business in Paris," Aragon said. "I'll give your problem some thought. I'm sure we'll come up with some intriguing options. Meanwhile, I insist you take full advantage of what *our* club has to offer."

A shapely hostess breezed by Sam, and he could have sworn she patted his butt. "I think I can keep myself entertained," he said.

They exited the lounge, and Aragon led the way to the waiting elevator. "This is Monique," Aragon said, indicating the unsmiling woman Sam had seen on his way in. "She controls access to the lower level, but there's just one more requirement."

"Something else?" Sam had hoped to see the lower level tonight.

Monique gestured for him to enter, and then she instructed him to place his hand in a luminous dark green square next to the control panel. "Palm flat," she said.

It was a palm scanner.

"Once we have your biometrics logged into the computer," Monique said, "you'll be allowed to come and go as you please. It shouldn't take more than twenty-four hours."

Sam wasn't pleased, nor was he buying her biometrics gobbledygook. They were probably going to run a fingerprint check on him, too, which rarely took more than a few minutes, if you had no criminal record. For some reason he was being stalled; still there wasn't much he could do about it now.

With one bright flash of the scanner, Sam was done. He stepped out of the elevator, and Aragon stepped in, probably intending to visit his office, said to be on the lower level. "We'll continue our chat when I return," he said. "Until then, enjoy. Any special requests, ask Angelic."

As the doors closed on Jason Aragon, Sam nodded a warm and friendly farewell, all the while thinking, *it won't be long now, you arrogant bastard.*

ALLY HESITATED in the lobby of the Hotel Lafayette, wishing she could turn and leave as swiftly and silently as she'd entered. She'd come to search a man's room, yet that wasn't what had stopped her. It was her memories of this place. She'd been here just the day before to set up this mission, but she'd been able to keep the past at bay until now.

The lobby buzzed with elegant guests. Its marble pillars and domed ceiling had always reminded her of the rotunda of a state building. However, today its grandeur made her feel disheveled and dirty. Her skirt was off-kilter, and she'd just noticed a smear of red clay ground into the hip.

She took cover near a potted palm and brushed at the fabric, trying not to be too obvious. Her best suit! She'd ruined it. The emotions flooding her had little to do with her clothing. This was the hotel where her mother and father had stayed when they'd come to New Orleans to save her from a fate worse than death—ruining the family name.

"Miss, is there something wrong? Can I help you?" a perturbed young man in red livery asked her. Although he had enough brass on his uniform to command an army, he was likely just a hotel clerk.

"No, I'm fine," she said, hoping her nerves didn't show. "I have a spot on my skirt. Is there a ladies' room nearby?"

He looked as if he wanted to hustle her out the back door. He obviously thought she was an interloper, maybe even a hooker. She'd love to tell him who she really was and blow his mind, but he'd never believe her. She was wearing a dirty suit with a miniskirt and a plunging neckline—of course, he wouldn't believe her.

"Down that hallway to your right, miss."

"Thank you." Ally squared her shoulders, proceeding with as much dignity as she could muster, which should have been considerable. Grace under fire had been drilled into her as child. In her parents' eyes, decorum was everything, as important as breathing.

She knew the clerk was watching her, and fortunately, the ladies' lounge was out of his eyeshot. *Un*fortunately, there was an attendant on duty in the lounge, and the woman's reaction was even more disapproving than the clerk's. Her grimace made Ally cringe.

Ally had planned to clean herself up at one of the sinks, but instead she locked herself in the nearest stall and used water from the toilet. Not one of her finer moments. As she dabbed the clay specks from her skirt, she almost wished the clerk had tried to throw her out. Maybe then she would have told him that her parents had once been guests in the presidential suite, and if pedigree mattered so much, he might like to know she was actually a princess.

Of course, he might not be so impressed with a royal family who'd been exiled and had their holdings seized by a cabal of despots. If Ally's parents hadn't had Swiss accounts, they would have been destitute. As it was, they'd been able to live a comfortable life and set up trusts for both their daughters.

The attendant knocked sharply on the stall door. "What are you doing in there?"

"What do you think I'm doing?" Ally bent over and flushed the toilet to make her point. The attendant retreated, and Ally did the best she could with her outfit. Moments later, armed with a haughty look, she came out of the stall, gave the woman a five-dollar bill and told her to keep the change. She swung through the lounge door and strode across the lobby, making sure the clerk saw her leave. She didn't stop walking until she was out of the hotel and in the parking lot, safe from prying eyes.

Okay. Now what, genius?

She was trembling by the time she got to her car. She couldn't very well have gone up to Sinclair's room after drawing so much unwanted attention. And if she'd had a choice, she would have been on a plane back to her apartment in Georgetown that night. The hotel brought back the all-night ordeal with her parents, every heartrending moment of it. They'd begged her not to tarnish the family name by getting involved with someone as notorious as Aragon. Their real mission, however, had been to persuade her to return to London and marry the man they'd chosen for her, a wealthy industrialist who could restore the Danner riches and their position in society.

The pressure on Ally had been intense, and it had started when she was seventeen and about to graduate from Alderwood. Her father had called, insisting she leave school and come to London to plan her own wedding. The prospect had struck horror in her heart, but she'd promised to return if he would let her graduate. He'd agreed, and she'd returned, prepared to do her duty, but she hadn't expected her betrothed to be an overbearing man in his midfifties, whose ideas about marriage were even more antiquated than her parents, and who would furtively grope and paw her under the table on their first dinner date. The bastard had wanted some return on his investment before the deal was done.

Ally pleaded with her father to call off the wedding, but couldn't make him understand that such an arrangement would never work for her. Desperate, she ran away, back to the States, where she worked her way through college by waitressing, and then, to ensure that she could never be forced into marriage, she devised a plan to "ruin" herself and become unacceptable to anyone else her father might choose. Jason Aragon had proved to be the perfect choice. She'd met him in New Orleans during spring break, never suspecting that he would become an even more dangerous trap than the one she'd escaped.

*And now he had her sister.*

Vix was paying the price for Ally's mistakes, and Ally had to get her back safely. She couldn't live with herself if she didn't, but how could she get up to Sinclair's room? She remembered a back elevator to the presidential suite that might open up on the other floors as well. The staff used it to deliver room service or whatever was needed to the suite. Now, if she could just find it without being spotted.

# 3

ALLY COULD SEE the headline now: Jail time for princess nabbed for breaking and entering. Glancing down at the stain on her skirt, she saw that she'd rubbed bits of white toilet paper into the red clay. Charming. All she needed was an ankle tattoo. Maybe a coiled snake or some lovely barbed wire.

Was she really going to do this?

She'd entered the hotel through a back entrance and found the staff elevator without being noticed. As she rode up to Sinclair's room on the fifth floor, doubts assailed her. She hadn't broken any laws yet. It wasn't a crime to follow a person as long as he didn't slap a restraining order on you. But breaking into his hotel suite while he was away?

Her mouth tasted gritty. Her nerves had been a jangled mess for days, and lack of sleep didn't help. Worrying about Vix had kept her awake all night. She didn't know where or how her sister was being held, whether she was being abused, or even if she was alive. Ally had checked her e-mail on her BlackBerry several times, but there'd been no messages from her sister.

Vix had been traveling on her own since she was a child. A short hop to New Orleans was nothing to her. She'd made the trip to check out Tulane University's undergrad program, and she'd been gone overnight when Ally had received that ominous e-mail from her. Ally had immediately called the hotel where Vix had planned to stay, but she hadn't checked in. There wasn't even a reservation for her.

Then Ally had called Vix's close friends in Georgetown, being careful not to alarm them when she asked about her sister. None of them had heard from Vix since she'd left. Reluctantly, Ally contacted the rock musician her eighteen-year-old sister had been dating, only to learn that he'd received an e-mail from Vix the same day Ally had. He'd revealed that Vix's e-mail had been upbeat and cheerful, and she hadn't mentioned any concerns beyond her choice of schools. Ally had doubts about her sister's boyfriend, but she had no reason to think he would lie about something like that. That was when Ally had decided to fly to New Orleans to check things out for herself.

Ally feared Vix might have gone to Club Casablanca out of curiosity. It was only a short drive from Tulane. She suspected her sister was fascinated with Jason Aragon because of the stories Ally had told her. She hadn't been trying to intrigue her sister, just the opposite. She worried that Vix would make the same mistakes she had, and she'd wanted her to understand that impulsive decisions could do lasting damage. But her impetuous sister had found Ally's walk on the wild side highly intriguing, and Vix had a rebellious streak, too.

She knew Jason Aragon to be capable of many things, but she didn't believe him evil enough to kill or even to take sexual advantage of her little sister. It was much more likely that he was using Vix as a means to an end, and that end was Ally, herself. Ally was the catch, Vix the bait.

He'd become controlling and obsessive, refusing to let Ally go when she wanted out of the relationship. At first she'd found his fast-paced, sexy lifestyle exciting, but it had frightened her when his physical desires began to darken, and she never got used to the leering club members who considered the hostesses free game. Not her, of course. She was Aragon's woman. No one touched her. But she didn't want Vix exposed to any of that.

When the elevators door opened, Ally took a moment to orient herself. The first thing she had to do was find the chambermaid she'd persuaded to help her. Ally had offered the young woman cash, but she'd refused it. She hadn't agreed to help until Ally disclosed that her sister was missing, and she was afraid for her safety. The chambermaid had lost her own sister to guerrilla forces in Guatemala, where she was born, and she'd been touched by Ally's plight.

Following the room numbers, Ally quickly located the one she wanted. She was relieved to see the maid already there, industriously polishing the brass doorknob and escutcheon. She spotted Ally, gave her a nod and opened the door to Sinclair's room.

"Hurry now!" the woman whispered as Ally slipped into the room. "You have five minutes, that's all. If anyone comes in, I'll lose my job, and you'll go to jail."

"Five minutes, and I'll be out," Ally promised, easing the door closed behind her. They'd agreed that the maid would remain outside to head off anyone who might show up, whether the hotel staff or Sinclair himself.

Ally swept the sitting room area, going through the drawers of the entertainment unit and the desk. She found nothing except the usual hotel stationery and sightseeing guides.

Next, she went through the entry closet, checked the guest bath and wet bar, and then lifted all the furniture cushions. As she worked, she noticed that every light in the place was burning. Sinclair hadn't bothered to turn them off. She made a mental note to keep her hands off the switches—she didn't want to give away that someone had been there.

Another thing she noticed as she moved through his suite was that other than a few toiletries and the expensive clothes hanging in the master closet, the place was as spartan and spotless as if unoccupied. That didn't make sense. You couldn't stay for any length of time in a hotel and not leave some trace of your presence—a scribbled note by the phone, an appointment book on the desk, pictures of family by the bed, a pay stub in the trash can. Something!

Unless you didn't want anyone to know who you were.

The maid had told her Sinclair's name, as well as ferreting out a few other details, like his profession. Ally needed more information. Much more.

She checked her watch as she entered the bedroom. The closet door was open, the light burning inside. As she darted over there, she had the craziest thought. Was this man afraid of the dark? Or was he expecting someone?

She fished through the pockets of the suit jackets that hung in the closet. Her efforts produced two sticks of Dentyne and the princely sum of forty-eight cents in loose change. She felt an odd tingle in the pit of her stomach and realized it was the gum. She would have thought it was nerves, except that the scent of cinnamon always reminded her of Red Hots candy, which had the strangest effect on her. Her first summer crush had been eating the candies when he kissed her mouth and a few other places, too. He'd left hints of the spicy scent on her breasts, and it had sent shivers through her days later. She'd refused to shower.

Ally figured that had to be the reason, but whatever it was, Red Hots made her hot. She held the gum to her nose and breathed in. Quickly she put the gum and the money back and cleared her thoughts. There was still work to do here. Her time was almost up, and she needed to know who Sam Sinclair was. In the most basic terms, was he a good guy or a bad guy? Could he be trusted? Would he help her or would he rat her out to Aragon? Those were the questions. But there were no answers in this suite. She stepped out of the closet, jerking her hand back seconds before she touched the light switch.

Her first criminal act was a bust, she realized as she returned to the living room. Worse, she didn't know where to go from here. She couldn't approach Sinclair knowing so little about him. But right now, she had to get out of the suite unseen. With the maid acting as lookout, that should be the easiest part of the night.

Voices? Ally crept into the foyer to listen. It sounded as if the maid were talking to someone outside. Ally hoped it was another hotel employee.

"How are you, Mr. Sinclair?" the maid said, speaking loudly enough for Ally to hear her. "I was just going to turn down your bed. I'm afraid we forgot to do that this evening."

"Thanks," Sinclair said, "but I'm exhausted."

"It's no problem, Mr. Sinclair. Really." The maid was nearly shouting now, and Ally had already backed out of the foyer.

"No thanks. I'll take care of it myself."

Ally's heart lost a beat when she heard Sinclair's reply. A second later the doorknob jiggled…then turned.

SAM DETECTED a faint scent the moment he opened the door to his room. Not perfume exactly, but intuition told him it was feminine essence. Light floral tones with a note of something else. Cinnamon? Maybe that determined little brunette who'd been following him for days had finally decided to sneak into his room. He'd left the lights on for her—that was a courtesy. He'd also moved his documents and his laptop computer to a safe place. That was a necessity.

As he slipped his key card into his pocket, it occurred to him that he could flush her out in ways that would probably blow her mind. But she wasn't a pro, he was certain of that, and there didn't seem any reason to scare the hell out of her. He'd already done that in the cemetery. Nor would he retrieve the small-frame 9 mm automatic he'd taped under the coffee table. It was there if he needed it.

Sam glanced around the living room as he headed for the bedroom. The lamp on the desk sat a few inches off, one of the sofa cushions was out of place, and he could see the indentation in the carpet where the trash container had been moved and resettled. Not bad for an amateur. It was a reasonably clean and thorough search, but a search nonetheless. But what was she looking for? And more importantly, who did she work for?

It was possible Aragon had sent her in to check him out. She might even be the reason Sam had been stalled in his access to the lower level, although Aragon wouldn't have been likely to use an amateur. Sam could feel his neck tightening at the thought of this woman in Aragon's employ. And it wasn't pleasure burning in his gut. No woman should be at the mercy of that bastard, and this woman didn't strike him as the type who'd let herself be at anyone's mercy. Maybe that's what drew him. Her nerve.

Hell, she was stalking him. That alone was pretty gutsy.

He couldn't think who else might want to investigate him at the moment, so the odds were with Aragon. This might be another test of Sam's suitability for membership, and he couldn't take the chance that it wasn't. Other than his uncle, no one knew about his personal reasons for being here, so she couldn't possibly be connected with that mess. If nothing else, he would get some answers out of her tonight.

Sam removed his leather jacket, threw it over the back of a chair and walked into bedroom. "Well, well, well," he said, eyeing his visitor.

Finding her had never been in question. Finding her draped across his king-size bed, her shoes kicked off and her chin propped up in her palm…now that was a bit of a surprise.

"Mr. Aragon sends his regards," she said, allowing a seductive pause before adding softly, "and me."

"Does he now?"

She nodded, her dark eyes sparkling as seductively as the tiny smile on her luscious lips. "I found my contact lens, thank you."

Sam made his way slowly to the side of the bed. "I'm glad to hear it." When he looked down, he spotted her high heels lying on the carpet, where she had kicked them off. "And just what am I supposed to do with you?" he asked.

He leaned against the dresser and crossed his arms over his chest. He gave her his best disarming smile as he cocked his head appraisingly.

"Anything you want."

"Now that's what I call a generous offer."

His focus narrowed on her face as he searched for something that he had seen a thousand times on a thousand different faces. It was called a tell, and every one had one. It could be anything—a tick, a cough, a certain glance, a gesture.

The woman on his bed locked stares with him. He wouldn't have called it a poker face, but she wasn't giving anything away. Or was she? His gut caught the nuance more than his eye. It wasn't much, a slight challenging rise of her left eyebrow.

"You're under no obligation," she said smoothly. "If you prefer to be alone, that's fine, too." She moved to sit up.

This was the preamble to her exit line, Sam knew. He pushed himself off the dresser and sat down on the side of the bed, deliberately taking in a long, leisurely eyeful of her. Her short skirt revealed a lot of leg, probably more than she wanted. But everything about those legs was sexy and nice, from her trim ankles to the curves of her calves and thighs. Even the goose bumps.

She was either cold or frightened. Probably both, he imagined. Personally, he liked it cold. It kept him sharp.

"No," he said, "I think I'd like you to stay a while. After all, it's rude to refuse a gift offered in friendship."

Sam rose and placed his hands on her shoulders. He gently pushed with one hand and pulled with the other, pivoting her around on her bottom until he had her positioned just so. He urged her back until her head rested on the thick, fluffy pillows. A strained smile fluttered across her lips as he brushed the hair from her forehead.

"So, how long have you worked for Mr. Aragon?" he asked. He kept his voice soft and nonthreatening.

"A while," she replied.

"Do you like your work?"

"Sometimes."

"Have you lived here long?"

"Not really."

Sinclair grinned. "You're just a font of information, aren't you? You sound a little dry. Would you like something to drink? Water, wine?"

She shook her head.

"Good, let's talk."

"About what?"

"I have to admit I'm curious about what took you into the cemetery late at night."

"Just taking a walk. I needed some air and I like dark places."

"I see," he said. "This walking through graveyards on your hands and knees...is that something you do often?"

"Not unless I lose a contact lens."

She compressed her lips in an effort not to smile that struck him as charming. "But you found it?"

"My brown eyes are blue tonight, aren't they?"

"Oh, yes." Another challenging tilt of her eyebrow. Possibly she was enjoying this match of wits as much as he was.

"You shouldn't sneak up on a girl like that," she said. "You startled me."

"And that's why you tried to hide from the security guards?"

Her brows knit. "I wasn't hiding, Mr. Sinclair. I was...I was startled. You frightened me, popping up out of nowhere like that. You shouldn't do that. In some circles it would be considered very rude."

"You seem pretty good at popping up out of nowhere yourself."

Her response was one of the best I-have-no-idea-what-you're-talking-about expressions he'd ever witnessed. And he'd witnessed a few.

Sam allowed silence to fill the seconds as he leaned toward her lips. "I'm going to kiss you," he said. "Is that all right with you?"

Her breath was warm on his cheek and smelled faintly of peppermint. But the tantalizing hints of cinnamon swirled around him, too. Was that her makeup? Her lipstick? He took in a deep draught, savoring its essence. She had to be one of the more enticing women he'd ever had on his bed. Too bad this was all just a setup on his part, a prelude to his interrogation process.

Her lips trembled slightly as his descended toward them. Sam took his time, and sweet time it was as he slipped his right hand under the fold between the pillows and the comforter. His fingers touched a cool, hard cylinder just as his lips touched warm, soft flesh. She moaned softly into his mouth, and Sam wasn't sure if it was protest or surrender.

He noticed she kept her hands at her side, her palms pressed tight against the bed as her entire body stiffened, becoming as rigid as a wooden plank. Before freeing her mouth completely, Sam indulged in a tiny nibble of her bottom lip. It was succulent and moist, sweet and lickable. Everything a bottom lip should be.

The sigh that slipped out of her was hot and breathy,

almost a moan. Sam knew if he didn't stop this he'd have his own wooden plank to worry about. The sensations stirring deep in his groin were all too familiar. Warmth and fullness. Rising male pleasure.

"Let's play a game," he whispered in her ear.

"Ga-ame?" Somehow she'd managed to stretch the word into two complete syllables and make it sound cute in the process. His wait for the proverbial gulp went unrewarded, however. All he got was a dry click from her throat. It would have to do.

He placed his left hand next to her right arm, letting his visitor know that he could easily pin her to the bed under him. As it was, they both understood that she wasn't going anywhere.

"It's been my experience that women either love this game or hate it," he said. "Nothing in between. What do you say? Don't want to disappoint Mr. Aragon, do we? Not when he was kind enough to send such a generous and alluring gift."

She kept trying to smile, and failing. "I suppose not."

"Good girl," Sam said. With that he pulled the cylinder from beneath the pillow, leveraged it with his knee and expertly ripped off a strip of silver tape, one-handed.

"What's that?" Ally asked.

She barely had the question out before her wrist was wrapped in silver. He held up the roll of duct tape for her to see, and she edged away from him.

"What are you going to do with that?"

It would have amazed her to know all the various uses a man like Sam had for duct tape, including de-linting his clothes and flinging it like a Frisbee to startle intruders. Right now, he had something more interesting in mind.

"I have enough of this stuff to wrap your entire naked body," he told her. "Quite a gift you'd be then, hmm? Can you imagine what that would feel like, especially when I unwrap you?"

He gave the tape around her wrist a tug, and then ripped it free. She winced, but held his gaze like a trooper. Still she was nervous now, and that was just where he wanted her. It was nothing personal. Situations like this demanded that he press his advantage.

"Is this a bondage game?" she asked. "I don't normally do the kinky stuff. I could get someone else for you, though. Just let me make a phone call, and I'll take care of that right away."

Sam smiled down at her as he stood up. "Bondage game? No, afraid not, although that might be interesting for later. What we're about to play is a mind game. And just so you know, there's a part of this game that some women simply hate."

Letting that sink in, he added, "I'm going to ask you some questions and you're going to answer them. There's nothing to it, as long as you tell me the truth, the whole truth and nothing but the truth. You're familiar with that concept, aren't you?"

The last question was delivered with a straight face.

The "ga-ame" had just turned serious.

WHY DID ALLY FEEL as if she'd just been asked the mother of all trick questions? Everything about the situation suddenly seemed like a setup. The lights being on, the absence of any personal items, Sinclair's unexpected appearance—had he known she would show up here?

Clearly the plan had blown up in her face, and she

couldn't see any way to turn things to her advantage, but she wasn't giving up. She'd been caught in his suite, trapped in his bed, and she strongly suspected he hadn't been fooled into believing she was one of Aragon's women, sent up as a midnight snack. But she was sticking to her story.

"I really do need to make a call," she said evenly. "If I don't check in with the club, they'll try to reach me on my cell."

"Well, if they do, I'll answer for you and tell them you're much too busy to be disturbed. Now…for our little game."

Sinclair bent down, picked up one of her high heels and held it up to the light, as if to examine it. She'd chosen the sexiest shoes she owned. They were open-toed with a cap heel and delicate straps that crisscrossed her ankle. But now they were scraped and soiled from her adventure in the graveyard.

He cast a quizzical glance her way. "Dirty shoes on an Aragon woman? By the looks of these heels, you must have taken the back way out of the cemetery. Wouldn't one of the club's hostesses change her clothes—and shoes— before making her appointed rounds?"

"I suppose I should have, now that you mention it. I didn't want to be late."

She didn't like where this was heading. He seemed to know more than he was letting on, which meant he was playing with her. She had to start planning her next move—out of this place.

Sinclair set down the shoe in favor of examining her ankles. He leaned across the bed and began tracing his fingertip along the tender flesh of her calves. "Goose bumps. Are you cold?"

*Ally* wasn't. She had too much adrenaline coursing through her body to feel the biting chill in the room.

"And these red bumps look like insect bites," he said. "Maybe chiggers? Mosquitoes? Just how long were you searching for your contact lens? Must have been quite some time."

Ally remembered being bitten by insects while at the cemetery. She hadn't thought it would be used as evidence against her.

"I'm not having fun," she said. "I'd like to go now."

"Oh, but I'm not through with you yet. In fact, we've only just started."

He sat down next to her, his smile fading as his dark eyes drilled holes through her. "I want to know why you're here and what you're up to," he said. "I'm not convinced you work for Aragon, or that he sent you here to please me or to keep me company. The game ends when I have those questions answered, and not a minute before."

He studied her intently. "And while we're at it, maybe you can explain why you've been following me for the last three days."

He had known all along. He had been just waiting for the right moment. The adrenaline blast that had cut off her ability to feel cold in the room was now paralyzing her vocal chords. "F-following you? No, I—"

Sinclair rose to his full height, gazing down at her. This time he meant business. His dark gold eyebrows had flattened and his expression was steely.

Ally ran through her options. She could tell him the truth, which was out of the question since she still wasn't sure who he was. Lie to him, which was tempting except that she didn't happen to have a convincing lie handy. Or remain silent and tell him nothing.

She went for the last one. Silence. Let him make the next move, she decided. If things got out of hand, she would scream her head off. This was a hotel. They had security.

"I'm waiting," Sinclair said.

"I must admit, you have me curious, Mr. Sinclair, if I may call you that. The club gave me your name. Maybe we can do some bargaining? I'll answer your questions if you answer mine."

Sinclair shook his head. "This is my game, and I don't answer questions."

"Then I don't play."

He cocked his head slightly. He was appraising her again, but Ally had no clue what was going through his mind.

His voice dropped low. "Remember when I said there was a part of this game that some women hated?"

She managed a weak nod, her heart thrumming wildly as he moved to the side of the bed. He pulled her to her feet, his fingers firmly wrapped around her wrists. "Well, here it comes."

# 4

SAM RELEASED Ally almost as swiftly as he'd pulled her to her feet. With a suspicious eye, she watched him reach for the phone on the nightstand.

"What are you doing?"

"Making a phone call."

He might as well have pulled a gun on her. Who was he calling? The police? Jason Aragon? She couldn't let him do either.

"Let's play that game," she said.

He cast her a quizzical glance. "Now you *want* to play?"

"I love games. Love, love, love them. Who doesn't? Put down the phone and let's play."

"Oh, but I can't. The phone call is an important part of this game."

"How so?" She didn't like the smile that played at the edges of his mouth. It was too sensual.

Sam tapped the receiver, probably to taunt her. "Ever played truth or dare? Well, this is truth or bare. I ask a question, and you answer it. If you tell the truth, we go to the next question. If I catch you in a lie, you remove one piece of clothing."

"Truth or bare?"

He rolled right on, ignoring her disbelief. "If you refuse to remove said piece of clothing, I pick up this phone, call Mr. Aragon, and tell him I'm not happy with my little gift."

He let that sink in before continuing. "There may even be time to return my gift to him personally, if that becomes necessary. Is there any part of the game you don't understand?"

He held out the phone, and she glared at him until he returned it to the cradle. She watched with annoyance as he fished around in his pocket and withdrew a handful of items. Among the keys and coins was an opened package of Dentyne.

Clearly the man had a bad gum habit.

Then she noticed the sparkly thing in his palm. Nestled next to the Dentyne was a small single key. She would have recognized it anywhere. The platinum key was the club's most coveted symbol of privilege. He now had access to the lower level, and that meant she needed him more than ever.

She hoped the urgency she felt didn't show. He'd done it. Somehow, he'd worked his way into the dark heart of Aragon's club. Keep a cool head, she told herself. Get some answers.

"First question." Sam returned the odds and ends to his pocket and popped a piece of the gum into his mouth. "What's your name? Your real name. The one on your birth certificate."

He seemed to be very intently searching her features. Let him look. She could bluff with the best of them. She'd lived in a fishbowl as a member of the royal court. A trip to the store had been a public appearance. She'd smiled and been gracious, always, even when she was coming apart inside.

Sinclair might think he had the upper hand with his duct tape and superior strength, but she knew more about him than he knew about her, which gave her the edge. Besides, she could say anything. How would he know she was lying? And the first lie had to be her name. She couldn't reveal her true identity to him as long as there was a chance he'd call Aragon.

"Diana Kelly," she said, stringing together the names of the last century's two most well-known princesses. She thought it was rather clever, but Sinclair was already shaking his head.

"That will cost one piece of clothing," he said. "I'll let you pick it."

"Gee, thanks. What makes you think that's not my name?"

"You hesitated before you said it. How many people hesitate when asked their name?"

"I wasn't sure I wanted to reveal it to you."

"That's another lie." He moved toward her.

"It is not!"

He kept coming. "And another," he said.

"All right, stop it now. You couldn't possibly know whether I'm lying or not."

She threw up her hands, but he stepped right past her barrier. "I not only know," he said, lightly stroking her eyebrow and the outline of her lips, as if this were show-and-tell, "I know it before you do. People who are about to lie glance to the left before they speak. You're textbook. You do it every time."

Ally felt as if the floor had given way beneath her. He was too close and too good at this. He didn't seem to know the meaning of personal space, and she couldn't stop him from invading  hers. Look at how he'd just helped himself to her mouth, as if it were a serving of dessert. Kissing it, touching it. What was he going to do with it next? Her lips felt hot and tender.

What had that damn ghost said? The ghost with *his* eyes. *These lips are mine?* Ridiculous. Who said things like that anymore?

Ally met his dark, burning gaze. She wouldn't let herself look anywhere else, but it was almost painful. It probably made sense that he knew how to spot a liar. He was a high-stakes gambler, and they won or lost on their ability to recognize a bluff. That might account for his skill, but he was much more than just a gambler.

This wasn't the time to confront him with her suspicions, she reminded herself. She had proof that he was running surveillance on the club, but she still didn't know whether he was a good guy or a bad one. If it was the latter, and he decided she knew too much, she might never have the opportunity to glance to the left again.

"Are you going to strip?" he said. "Or should I start dialing?"

Her silence prompted him to pick up the phone and tap out the club's numbers. "Angelic?" He spoke into the receiver. "This is Sam Sinclair. Would you be good enough to put me in touch with—"

"Okay, okay. You've made your point." Ally snatched the phone out of his hand and hung it up.

She could almost feel the dark smile behind his narrowing eyes.

"That's more like it," he said. "What's your name?"

"Britney Spears." She mentally stuck out her tongue at him.

"I'd say that qualifies as another lie. How many is that? I've lost count." He reached for the phone again, and Ally let out a yelp.

"Hey, I was just kidding!"

"I'm *not*." He waggled his index finger at her clothing. His meaning was clear.

Pervert, she thought, taking silent inventory of what she was wearing—a suit jacket and skirt, camisole, bra, panties and hose. That amounted to six lies before she'd be nude, and she wasn't sure how many she'd told already. But she also had a hair clip, watch and bangle bracelet, which could stretch it out to nine.

If there was ever a time to get good at lying, it was now.

"Okay, I'll play your silly game." She removed the hair clip.

"Nice try," Sinclair said as her hair fell onto her shoulders, "but that doesn't count. Accessories aren't clothes. If you won't pick it, I will. Lose the jacket."

A moment ago he was a pervert. He'd just been promoted. "Sicko," she muttered as she took off her cropped suit jacket.

Sinclair shrugged. "I've been called worse."

"I'm sure you have." She tossed the jacket onto the bed and shivered. She seemed to have lost her immunity to the cold temperature of the room. Her silk camisole felt like ice against her flesh. Thank God she'd worn a bra. The last thing she needed was her nipples reacting to the chill. Now *that* would be sending the wrong signal.

To his credit—if the man was worthy of any—Sinclair didn't gawk at her. His dark gaze brushed over her bare shoulders, making her feel as if she'd been illicitly touched. *When wasn't he illicitly touching her?* But other than that, he simply folded his arms, and it was business as usual.

"We'll come back to the name," he said. "Why have you been following me for the last three days?"

"I haven't been following you. I don't even know you. Jason Aragon sent me."

He chuckled lightly. "I can see this is going to get interesting. Remove something."

"Why? I didn't glance to the left." In fact, she'd glanced to the right, just to be sure.

"You think that's the only way to spot a liar? There are dozens of nonverbal signals associated with lying, and you've had all the clues you're going to get. May I suggest the skirt?"

He popped his gum, and Ally thought of Red Hots candy. Her lips tingled. *Not now.*

"What are you, a psychologist?" she said. "A profiler?"

"You have no idea," he said.

She had an idea. She had several ideas about him—and no intention of taking off any more clothing. Too bad she couldn't back him off with what she knew about him, but there was too much at stake. She was the only one who knew Vix was missing, so it was entirely up to her. If she messed this up, she didn't want to think about what might happen to her sister.

Ally could read signals, too, and she was fairly certain sex wasn't one of Sinclair's goals in getting her naked. She'd already draped herself across his bed invitingly, but he hadn't taken her up on it. No, he wanted information, and this was his way of scaring her into giving it up.

Actually, maybe she would give it up—not information or sex, but another piece or two of clothing couldn't hurt.

It would buy her some time and possibly get her the information she needed. And if it got her sister back, she'd undress to the buff and dance a jig.

Let's see. What could she take off next without giving away the farm? From what she knew of the club, an Aragon girl wouldn't have all that much trouble stripping, and Ally still had hopes of convincing him she *was* one of those girls, but she had no desire to get herself into any more trouble.

She glanced his way as she hiked up her skirt to remove her pantyhose. He was watching her with the cool detachment of a poker player, but she still felt vulnerable. He was so much bigger than she was. And meaner.

"You could at least be a gentleman and turn around."

"Sorry, the last thing I need is you banging me over the head with a lamp."

"What a *brilliant* idea."

Fine, she thought. If he wouldn't turn around, she would.

She pivoted, giving him the full effect of her haughty stance. As quickly as possible, she shimmied out of her pantyhose. *There, that wasn't so bad.* But when she turned around, his skepticism had morphed into dark amusement. He was enjoying this too much.

He snapped his gum, and a blast of cinnamon flooded her air space. So rude. And why cinnamon, the very essence of Red Hots?

"If it hasn't dawned on you yet, I have far more questions than you have clothing," he informed her. "It's going to get awfully cold in here if you don't start telling me the truth."

"Bring it on." She tossed her balled-up pantyhose, and he snapped them out of the air. Excellent reflexes.

"Whatever you say, lady." He let his eyes drift down her

body, lingering on all those places that she most wanted to keep covered. And while he was so casually caressing her with his gaze, he rolled the pantyhose ball around in his palm, squeezing it occasionally.

*So* obvious. Go ahead, she told him with an expression of casual disdain, feel me up all you want, as long as you do it from over there. You're not going to rattle me. But she hadn't planned on having to watch him bring the nylons to his nose, as if he were drinking in the fragrance of sweet woman flesh, and then to his lips, as if he could taste her. And she hadn't totally accounted for the raking heat of his eyes, either.

She didn't want to react, but she could feel the warmth invading her skin. Damn, she could. It made her hot just thinking about being naked under his gaze.

Finally, he tossed the pantyhose on the bed, ready to move on to other things, apparently. She refused to flinch when he placed his fingertips on her throat. She could barely feel his touch, but even the feather-light contact had the sizzle and snap of a live wire. And wouldn't you know the man reeked of Red Hots.

God, how she secretly thrilled to that smell. It made her weak and infused her with energy at the same time. Exciting, but *confusing*.

"I know what you're doing," she said. "You're taking my pulse, right? This is part of your lie-detecting routine."

He was focused on her facial features, searching for something, and it wasn't for one of the signals of deception. In her experience when a man looked at a woman this way, he usually kissed her, and this man wouldn't stop there, she knew.

"Why are you afraid of Aragon?"

His question didn't really register. She'd been searching his face as he'd searched hers—and again, a sense of déjà vu had crept in. Was she supposed to know him from some place? She was haunted by a nagging sense that they'd met before—perhaps years before—but the details remained elusive.

"The silent treatment won't work," he said. "I asked you why you were afraid of Aragon."

"He'll fire me if you call him. You must know how he is."

"You don't work for Aragon any more than I do." He lifted his fingers from her neck. "You've done nothing but lie since we started the game. You're lucky I'm not a hard nose, or you'd be naked by now. Skirt or camisole?"

"*You're* not a hard nose?"

"Would you like me to be one? The camisole," he said. "You take it off or I will."

"You're a despicable man." Ally pulled the camisole over her head and threw it on the bed. "De*spicable*. I'm not surprised Jason likes you."

She was now down to her skirt and her bra. Charming.

He gave her cotton bra a long hard look. He was clearly curious, and apparently not bothered that the style was modest by today's standards. It resembled a sports bra. She wouldn't have called it sexy by any means, and yet, he seemed to think so.

She heard his deep breath and saw the speed with which his pupils had expanded. His dark brown eyes were turning midnight black.

He cleared his throat and spoke. "All you have to do is tell me the truth, and the game is over. You can get dressed. I'll *help* you."

Was that a note of panic in his tone? Ally wasn't quite sure what to do. She couldn't tell him the truth, but he hadn't missed a single lie so far. He might be bluffing, but even with the best odds, he should have stumbled at least once by now.

She needed to test him, but how?

"Tell me why you broke into my room."

"I did tell you," she insisted.

"And you lied."

Very deliberately—and with no warning or apology— he placed his hand over her heart. Obviously to check the rate. It was exactly where a physician would have placed a stethoscope, but this guy wasn't a physician, and Ally's heart happened to be conveniently located beneath her left breast, like every woman's.

The sudden intimacy of his touch made it hard for her to speak.

"Take your hand off my breast," she croaked.

He smiled, caressing her with his thumb. "Make me."

The intimacy was too much, the heat too fierce. She gripped his wrist, and he gripped hers.

"Let go of me," she whispered.

"The minute you let go of me."

"This is silly. Count of three and we both let go."

A slow headshake. "Count to three thousand, if you want. I could do this for hours—and will, unless you tell me the truth."

"I *didn't* break in." Her voice took on a pleading note. The truth, at least technically. But her damn fluttering pulse didn't seem to care whether she was being honest or not. And why wouldn't it with him fondling her breast?

His gaze grew darker by the moment. Whether or not

he believed she was lying, he wasn't letting up on the
pressure, either mentally or physically. His eyes searched
her, and his thumb feathered her hardening nipple. He
was clearly savoring the feel of her.

Now she couldn't even speak. She released his wrist,
and he released hers, thank God. He freed her, but she
could feel the imprint of his palm as if it were still there.
She could feel his fingers taking possession of her flesh,
and her face flushed with awareness.

"It's basic biology," he said, putting some effort into
keeping his voice unaffected. "Your pulse rate increases
when you lie, those pretty little pupils of yours react
when you lie and your body temperature fluctuates when
you lie. All measurable signals that will be used against
you in this game."

He'd opened the way for Ally. Observing him carefully,
she said, "You didn't get this good at reading people from
gambling. You're a professional, right? You do this for a
living? Maybe for the police? The FBI?"

He laughed. "I went to Catholic school. Ever wonder
why you can't lie to a nun and get away with it?"

"Now, *you're* lying. You didn't go to Catholic school.
Your eyes veered so far left they hit the curb. If you'd been
in a car, you would have had an accident."

He nodded approvingly. "You just proved my point.
Humans are conditioned to tell the truth, no matter what.
Our bodies react when we don't tell the truth, and there's
damn little we can do to control it."

"So, then, you *are* a cop?"

He raised a warning eyebrow. "What's it going to be?
Skirt or bra? Just holler if you need help with those bra
hooks."

"Aren't you the Boy Scout!" She averted her eyes and the room seemed to shimmer. It had been too long since she'd slept or eaten, and with the scent of Red Hots bathing her every time he spoke, she was getting lightheaded. She didn't seem to have the energy to argue with him. And really, what was the point? Her body let her down even when she was telling the truth.

She undid her skirt and let it fall to the floor, leaving her in nothing but her bra and panties. As she looked up, she saw that his expression had changed dramatically, but it wasn't what she expected.

He took a step back, clearly skeptical of what he saw.

"What's wrong?" she asked, stealing a quick look at herself. The panties were just everyday undies. Maybe not the sexiest lingerie in the world, but they were comfortable and practical, and she hadn't thought to bring anything else for this trip.

Sinclair was shaking his head. "Now I *know* you're not an Aragon woman. No way would he send someone here in underwear like that."

Ally wasn't buying it. "Some men find good-girl underwear very sexy." Like you, dude.

"Yeah, the perverts and sickos."

"I guess that makes you one of the above, based on your body language. When I took off my camisole your voice got hoarse, your eyes dilated and if I'd touched your throat, I'm sure I would have felt a thunderstorm in there."

She couldn't accuse him of an erection because she hadn't thought to look down. "You said we couldn't control our reactions, and you did react. You're reacting right now."

She reached over to feel his pulse, and he snapped her into his arms and whipped her around. His fingers curled around the band of her bra, and she felt a sudden release of pressure. He'd unhooked the bra, but he was holding it together, ready to expose her. That wouldn't have bothered an Aragon girl for a second.

"The truth," he said. "Why the hell are you here?"

Ally's heart was off the scale again. If they'd been playing poker, he would have held the winning hand by virtue of his bad-ass attitude alone, but she hadn't played her ace yet. It would be dangerous, but she might even be able to force Sinclair to ante up some information.

"It's your choice," he said. "A call to Aragon is the fastest way to get this settled."

"By all means," she said, "call him."

He walked to the phone and picked it up. Ally clutched the bra to her breasts. She knew he'd do it this time. It was now or never.

"I can tell him about *you* while we're at it," she said.

His eyebrows formed a threatening V. "What about *me?*"

Ally pressed her advantage. "I'm sure he'd like to know that an undercover cop has infiltrated his inner sanctum. Jason doesn't like cops, unless they're on his payroll. Maybe you are, but I strongly doubt it."

If her words shocked him, he covered it up well. The phone found its way back to the cradle. She tilted her head, challenging him to disagree. When he didn't, she allowed herself a faint smile. Maybe she should make *him* answer some questions, strip him naked if he lied to her. If nothing else, she was certainly going to let him sweat for a moment or two. He'd earned himself that much discomfort.

SAM ENJOYED surprises about as much as he enjoyed sucker punches to the gut. He'd spent the better part of his life learning how to read people for the sole purpose of *avoiding* surprises. Had, in fact, paid his way through college with his winnings at the poker table. And here, this fascinating little brunette had come damn close to making him in less than an hour. He was impressed.

Unfortunately she now posed a real threat to his mission. He had to regain control and fast.

"What makes you say that?" he asked.

"Because it's true. All the evidence points to it. You're either in law enforcement setting up a sting or you're a gangster out to get even with Jason." She shook her head, a faint smile touching her sensual lips. "And you're no gangster."

"Evidence?" Sam's voice had taken on a nonchalant tone as if he could care less about her conclusions. In reality, he cared deeply. If she had uncovered the truth, then Aragon could do the same.

"This hotel suite, for starters. Look at it. Nothing here reflects that a real live person is a guest here."

"I'm real. I'm alive," he said.

"Exactly, and that's my point. There's nothing here because you're hiding your identity. What about those mysterious phone calls you make, always away from the hotel as if you're afraid you might be overheard? And the surveillance equipment you keep hidden in that abandoned car in the woods?"

What the hell had she been up to? "You lied about following me. You just admitted it."

Her show of bravado faded slightly as her eyes took on a distant look that Sam had seen a thousand times. Do I bet, bluff or fold? That's what she was asking herself, and it was the sign of a weak hand. She wasn't out of the game, but she was debating a hand that wasn't the winner she'd thought.

The suite was so quiet Sam could actually hear her breathing. As the seconds crawled by, he fought the urge to watch her breasts rise and fall with her breathing. It shocked him that such prissy underwear could turn him on. Maybe he *was* a sicko, but the way she was trying to cover her gorgeous boobs with that white scrap of a bra was unbelievably sexy.

He couldn't go there. It would cost him his edge. It might even cost him his life—or hers, for that matter—but the urge was there. He wanted to rip that silly thing out of her hands and leave her topless and shaking... topless and shaking in his arms.

Soft skin. Bare breasts filling his hands. Hot lips, kissing his mouth and every other damn place a man dreamed about.

He forced himself to concentrate on her eyes—and realized he'd made another mistake. Some women had eyes that seduced. This one's eyes could hijack a man's imagination and reduce him to a babbling idiot. Erotic and exotic, they were tilted like marquise-cut gems. But there was something else lurking in those lovely dark orbs besides her God-given sensuality.

Fear and desperation.

Whoever she was, she was scared, which meant she was probably operating alone. His intuition had already told him that much. He knew from personal experience how dangerous it was to let down his guard, especially with a vulnerable woman, but he bet he had this one pegged.

"Am I right?" she said. "You're working for some law enforcement agency?"

"Am *I* right? You're not sent by Aragon?"

After what seemed like an interminable amount of time, she let out a deep, soulful sigh—and looked him straight in the eye.

"My name is Allegra Danner, and I need your help. If you're in law enforcement, I could be in big trouble. If you're not, I'm probably a dead woman."

# 5

"ALLEGRA DANNER," Sinclair said evenly, repeating her name.

There was no hint of recognition in his voice, which was the good news. Ally had already exposed her family to enough notoriety by working at Club Casablanca and being Jason Aragon's woman.

The bad news was she'd had to risk giving him her name, but there didn't seem to be any other way to make him believe her. Clearly she wasn't a convincing liar.

"My friends call me Ally. Can I put my clothes back on? The North Pole must be c-cozy compared to this place."

She'd anchored her unhooked bra in place with her crossed arms, but the room was truly freezing. Her lips were so cold she was having trouble talking.

"Not just yet."

"Why? I t-told you my name."

"I'm afraid there's more."

"In case you haven't noticed, and I'm sure you *h-have* noticed, there's not much left to take off."

She felt like a germ under a microscope around this guy. A cold germ. She didn't know whether he was searching for signs of deception or simply formulating his next move. At least his voice and countenance had softened slightly. He was less broodingly suspicious at the moment. She took that as a good sign.

"What kind of trouble are you in and how am I supposed to help you?" he said, taking a step back, as if for some kind of distance.

Fair enough questions, Ally thought. She'd been preparing herself to answer them ever since she realized she would need help in this mission. He was going to get the truth, maybe not all of it, but as much as she dared give him.

"I believe Jason Aragon is holding my sister Victoria against her will. As you know, female guests have to be escorted by a male member in good standing, which is why I'm here—and why I need you."

Sinclair's mouth twitched. "That's all you need? A good-standing male member? Why didn't you just say so?"

Penis humor. Ally was trying to rescue her sister, and he was making locker room jokes? She told herself humor was better than anger and suspicion. She told herself to be civil.

"Mr. Sinclair, I have to get my sister out of there before something terrible happens to her. Just get me past security," she said. "That's all I'm asking."

"Are you claiming that Aragon kidnapped your sister? Why would he do that?"

Ally hadn't intend to tell him everything about her relationship with Aragon. She would probably lose *all* credibility if he knew that she and the club owner had been lovers. Yet there was too much at stake not to make him see that her sister was in real danger.

"I received an e-mail from her telling me that Aragon was holding her prisoner at the club. Those were almost her exact words."

"An e-mail?" The brooding countenance made an encore, and it was particularly effective with his hard-edged features.

"Anyone with your e-mail address could have sent that to you," he pointed out. "Do you know how easy it is to fake an e-mail? How can you be sure it came from her?"

"She signed it with the nickname that I use for her, probably so that I would know it was her. She hates the nickname Vix. She's eighteen and considers it an embarrassment. I'm certain it was from her."

Ally sank to the floor and searched through the clothing she'd dropped. She'd tucked a printout of the message in an inner pocket of her skirt meant for cash and credit cards.

"Here," she said, handing it to Sinclair as she rose. "In case you're wondering, I've done some investigating. I've called our family, her friends, everyone I could think of. No one has any idea where she is."

Sinclair read the note aloud. "'I'm in trouble. Jason Aragon is holding me prisoner at his club. He hasn't hurt me. I'm afraid he will if you call the police. Please don't tell anyone. He has friends everywhere. He'll know! Ally, I'm so sorry! Vix.'

"This is all you have?" He dangled the paper. "What if it's a prank? Is your sister a practical joker?"

"My sister has *vanished.* Am I supposed to dismiss that as a joke? I need to get inside that club. I have to know if she's there or not."

Ally tweaked the note from his fingers.

"Sounds like you've contacted all the right people," he said, "Did you try calling the local police?" He wasn't being sarcastic this time. It was more a request for information.

"The police are out of the question. I have to do this on my own and you have to help me."

"That's a contradiction." The amused glint returned. Apparently that was how the man smiled, through his eyes—and it was always at her expense.

"You know what I mean," she said. "Now, please, I need an answer. Time may be running out for my sister." She was trying to forge an alliance, not alienate him, but he was making it difficult.

His smile had vanished. "I need some answers, too—and I'm going to get them before we take this any further. Now sit down, shut up and listen."

She sat down. She didn't appreciate his drill sergeant routine, but sat down anyway. It would have been foolish to do otherwise. Besides she had the feeling he was actually trying to make sense of the situation. How many times did an exiled princess break into a man's room, beg him for assistance in rescuing a kidnapped sister and do all of that while said princess was half-naked? Of course he didn't know about the royalty part. Even leaving that out, he probably didn't find himself in circumstances like this too often.

"You said you'd be a dead woman if I wasn't in law enforcement. What was that supposed to mean?" he asked her.

Ally shivered. She didn't know whether it came from the chilliness of his suite or his question. At least this time he responded to her distress with some concern. He went to a nearby chair, picked up a down throw and came back to the bed. Ally thanked him as he draped the material over her shoulders. Maybe he had a heart after all. Black as sin, no doubt, but a heart nonetheless.

"Better?" he asked.

*Anything* was better than freezing. Her nipples had

turned to diamonds, and her legs were shaking. She nodded her head, clutching the throw around her and hoping her bra would stay where it belonged.

"My sister's right about Aragon," she said. "He has lots of friends. Just for the sake of argument, let's say you were one of them, and you decided to tell him about me. That could put me in great danger. He might even decide to have me killed. All hypothetical, of course."

She raised her hand, signaling that she wasn't done. "On the other hand, if you were an enemy—say some criminal type here to kill Aragon—then you might feel you had to kill me to keep me quiet. But if you're neither of those things, if you're just a regular guy, and you tell anyone about me, word will get back to Aragon, and my sister and I will both be in danger."

She dragged in a breath. "So everything I've learned about you leads me to believe you're in law enforcement."

Ally studied him, determined to gauge his reaction. If the wrong signal came across—if her instincts told her she was in danger—she would run for the door and scream bloody murder on the way.

Sinclair could stonewall with the best of them. She didn't pick up anything, which was frustrating, given how easily he could read her.

He moved to the dresser and leaned against it, staring at her. "Why me? Of all the people in that club, why did I draw the winning ticket?"

"Well, when I saw you doing surveillance on the club I knew you weren't just another member—and quite honestly, there's something familiar about you."

His head lifted. She had piqued his interest. "Familiar? How so?"

"I don't know." She really didn't, but he would never accept that as an answer, she knew. "Okay, I admit this sounds crazy, but I dozed off in the graveyard last night, just for a second, but I had a dream about a ghost—and when I woke up, there you were, and I got confused."

"You thought *I* was a ghost? The one who haunts the graveyard? Micha Wolverton?"

Apparently that wasn't so crazy. He sounded defensive, as if she'd accused him of something. But of what—being a ghost? His voice had an edge to it that almost frightened her, but that was just too bizarre. There had to be some other explanation.

Ally shivered again. She couldn't seem to stop.

"I was confused," she said.

"Right, confused."

"And cold…it's so cold in here."

After a moment, he moved quietly from the dresser to the bed. He took the folded comforter and draped it over her arms and back. "Better?"

The warmth of his hands flowed over her icy shoulders as if it were a soothing balm. There was even heat coming through his clothing. She felt it along with his breath as he pulled the comforter tighter around her.

She closed her eyes, soaking it in. "Yes, much better."

It surprised Ally that she could allow herself to be this needful of his comfort. But she'd never been this desperate before. When he'd wrapped the soft down around her shoulders, cocooning her inside, she'd wished that for just a moment or two he was inside with her, sharing some of the amazing warmth emanating from him.

How bizarre, she thought, that she should be half-naked in a stranger's hotel suite, longing to steal some of his masculine heat, when all she really wanted—should want—was to be sure her sister was safe.

He didn't seem to pick up on any of this. He went back to his post at the dresser, settled against it and waited. There was no denying that he was determined to get some answers from her no matter how long it took.

"Do you believe in déjà vu?" she asked him. "Well, the feeling that I'd seen you somewhere before…it was like that."

"I believe in what I can see and what I can touch." Then, he added brusquely, "I believe in facts."

Ally stiffened. "Well, here's a fact. I need your help, Mr. Sinclair. I desperately need your help. And I can give you what you need in return."

"You're going to give me what I need?" He almost laughed. "How could you possibly know what I need? You're not even sure whether I'm a cop or a criminal."

"I know you're after someone or something inside that club."

"And you can help me with that?"

"Yes, I can. I know more about Club Casablanca than you can imagine." She did know some of the inner workings of the club, but Sinclair hadn't committed to helping her yet. If she told him her secrets, what was to keep him from getting rid of her and using the secrets himself?

She took another approach, equally dangerous.

"Here's a fact you can believe." She leveled her gaze at him. "I'm not the only one at risk here. Anyone crazy enough to spy on Jason Aragon for *any* reason is in grave danger. If he were to find out about you, your life wouldn't be worth much more than mine."

She'd just come very close to a blackmail threat.

Reckless, possibly, but she wanted him to know that the threat existed, and that she was capable of it.

She clutched the comforter tightly and rose from the bed. "I'll give you some time to decide if we have a deal," she said, stooping to pick up her skirt and hose. "I'll be in the other room."

She needed some breathing room. But more than that, she needed to know if he'd let her leave the room. Her plan was to move to more neutral space and to get her clothes back on…but she only got as far as the spot where her top had fallen.

"Hold it," Sinclair said, pushing off the dresser.

Ally's heart skipped painfully as he strode toward her, effectively blocking her off. "Don't even think about getting physical with me," she warned him, opening her robe enough to show him her cocked knee. "If you care about your cojones at all, Sinclair, don't even think about it."

SAM COULD HARDLY THINK of anything he'd like better, even at the risk of his cojones. Right now, getting physical with this strangely bumbling, strangely clever, strangely lovely female probably topped his list. Unfortunately, he had something even more pressing on his mind. Survival.

A part of him wanted to believe her, or at least give her the benefit of doubt. Her story was just wild enough that it might be true. But he'd caught her in so many lies he'd be a damn fool to trust her. And what on earth could a woman who wore white cotton underwear possibly know about the illicit and even dangerous dealings inside Jason's club?

One thing was certain. He couldn't allow her to walk out of here, not given what she knew about his clandestine activities at the club. If any of that got back to Aragon, his plans would be ruined, which, ironically, put him in the same leaky boat with her. She'd sworn they could help each other, but that wasn't reason enough to join forces with her. He needed information.

"Sit down," he said. "We aren't finished yet."

She sat on the foot of the bed, huddled in the comforter. Her fear was obvious, but he would have been more suspicious if she hadn't been apprehensive. What struck him was her look of quiet desperation. It made her face pale and her eyes dull. She seemed to be pretty good at hiding her inner, more complex emotions, but no one was a stone. And desperation usually meant that he was getting closer to the truth.

He took a step back, giving her some space and decreasing the threat of his nearness. Fear was a useful weapon, but too much could silence a person, and he needed answers. Of all the questions running through his head at the moment, one stood out above all the others. What if she were telling the truth? What if she did know something vital about Aragon's operation? And what if her little sister really was being held by that sick bastard?

Sam had no siblings. His mother had died while giving birth to him, leaving his grief-stricken father to raise him. His father had never been able to break the painful association of her death and Sam's birth.

And neither had Sam. He'd never had anything like a family, so it was impossible for him to understand the power of those ties, but he'd sure as hell known something was missing in his life. It may have been his longing for a real connection that had driven him into relationships with women needing rescue.

The first one had been the wife of his slain partner. Sam had been a rookie with the agency, and he'd been as devastated by the loss of his friend and partner as the wife had been by the loss of her husband. Sam had offered comfort and support. However, she'd taken it as something else. He'd been young. He hadn't known how to handle it.

The second woman had never stopped needing to be rescued, but Sam couldn't save her because she didn't want to be saved. She thrived on creating one drama after another. That realization had cured him. He'd told himself he didn't need an intimate relationship—and couldn't have one with the life he led. What was the point in longing for a close connection when you worked undercover? Always on the move, always looking over your shoulder. He was alone. It had to be that way.

Ally had that connection with her sister and didn't want to lose it. He couldn't even pretend to understand the level of her concern. If the tables were turned, though, and it was his sister being held hostage, he'd be willing to do anything to get her back safely. Just like the woman sitting on his bed.

*You don't have to have a relationship with her, Sam. Or even a one-night stand. Here's a thought: Maybe you can help her. Maybe she can help you.*

He drew in a breath. "Has there been any kind of ransom note or demands made in exchange for your sister?"

Her eyes got big, hopeful. It was almost enough to make him wish he'd kept his mouth shut. Christ, he was an idiot.

"No," she said. "Are you going to help me?"

"*I* ask the questions," he told her. Suddenly he was hot under the collar, even in this refrigerator of a suite. He took off his jacket and tossed it on the nearest chair. "If your parents got a ransom demand, would they tell you?"

"Yes, absolutely. Vix has been staying with me since she started school in the States. And, besides, the e-mail came to me, not to them."

"Tell me about her," Sam said. "Is she outgoing? Shy and retiring?"

Anger sparked in Ally's soulful eyes. "Vix is clever and very willful, but she's eighteen and no match for Aragon, dammit. I don't know why you can't understand that."

She caught herself. "I'm sorry," she said. "I'm frightened."

Sam understood her fear, and he felt for her. What did she expect him to do? Charge into the Club Casablanca with guns blazing and demand the release of a woman he wasn't even sure was being held there?

"It may not be a kidnapping," she said quietly. "At least not the way you're thinking."

Sam peered at her in disbelief. She'd just whipped him another curve ball. "Well, if it's not a kidnapping, what the hell is it?"

"She may have gone there on her own," Ally explained. "I don't think Jason or his thugs snatched her off the street, and I don't think this is about ransom money."

She sighed deeply, seemingly reluctant to go into details. Finally, she began to let it out. "It's about obsession," she said. "Dark, perverted obsession. That's my guess, anyway."

Sam waited for her to continue, aware as the seconds

ticked by that the more he learned about her the less he understood her. And he did seem to want to understand her, which should have been a red flag in itself, everything considered. It would have been easy to blame his strange attraction to her on a backlog of testosterone. He hadn't been with a woman in a very long time, and this one had that spark about her. That might even explain why her ridiculous white cotton undies had become a magnet to his imagination. But it was more than physical lust, he knew. And he wouldn't have ruled out admiration. She had guts. He'd never met anybody with guts quite like hers.

She glanced up at him. What she had to say wasn't coming easily.

"Years ago, I had a relationship with Jason," she explained. "He'd just taken over the club and had visions of turning it into a Mecca for wealthy VIPs from all over the world. I didn't know the full scope of what he had in mind, and I didn't care. I was young and foolish—and determined not to go through with the arranged marriage my family wanted."

Sam was careful not to react as she went on, telling him how she'd tried to ruin her reputation and discourage her wealthy fiancé. But he loathed the very thought that she'd been with Jason Aragon. It made him want to neuter the son of a bitch.

"At first I found Jason exciting and sophisticated," she said. "The club was glamorous and the costumes made me feel like a woman of mystery, a grown-up. But Jason grew increasingly demanding and controlling. He assigned a security guard to watch me, and sometimes he locked me up."

Ally shuddered, sinking into the comforter as if she

wanted to disappear. She seemed embarrassed, even hu-
miliated—and the flame-red color seeping into her cheeks
gave away the depth of her feelings. That was the moment
Sam realized that he believed her.

"My plan worked perfectly," she admitted. "My fiancé
broke it off, and my parents, who are European and very
old-fashioned, did everything but disown me. It was
exactly what I wanted at the time."

"You ran straight to Jason."

She nodded. "And in a way, I've been running away
from him ever since. I was with him two years. I finally
escaped during one of his costume balls by disguising
myself and walking out the front door."

"Your sister knew about all this?" Sam asked.

"No, she's ten years younger than I am. She was just a
kid at the time, living with my parents in London. When
she turned fourteen my parents sent her to Alderwood, a
boarding school in Georgetown, and she stayed with me
on weekends. I saw it as a chance to repair things with my
family. I promised my parents I'd keep an eye on her, but
the only thing Vix had on her mind was boys—and the
wrong kind of boys, of course. I couldn't make her listen
to reason, so I told her what had happened with Jason. I
just wanted her to learn from my mistakes. No sordid
details, of course, just enough to frighten her off…or so
I thought."

Finally she looked at him, clearly shaken by the story
she'd had to tell. "I may have made it sound exciting and
forbidden, but I didn't mean to."

Sam nodded that he understood. At least things were
beginning to make sense now. It was the classic contest
of wills—the younger sister rebelling against the older

one. That had a truer ring than Aragon kidnapping a young woman for no apparent reason.

Sam sat down beside her at the foot of the bed. "I'm going to help you, though not the way you suggested."

"What does that mean?"

"It means that I'll look for your sister when I go back into the club tonight. If I find her, I'll get her out, or at the very least, make sure she's okay. I'll tell her you're worried about her and that she needs to contact you. That's the best I can do."

Ally stared at him in shock. "I'm sorry, Mr. Sinclair," she said, flaring, "your best isn't good enough. You'll never find her on your own. You don't know where to go. You don't even know what she looks like. I *have* to go with you."

"Forget it," he said, his patience wearing thin.

So was hers, it seemed. Her eyes narrowed in cold defiance, and Sam knew he had a fight on his hands.

"Don't make me blackmail you, Mr. Sinclair," she said. "If I have to turn you over to Jason in order to free my sister, I will. I swear to you, I will."

# 6

---

"YOU'LL HAVE TO GET to Jason before I do," Sam told Ally quietly.

She was burning up with indignation. Her neck and shoulders were rigid, her expression fierce, but the emotions fueling her were much more complex than just outrage. He'd seen guilt, remorse, even shame in her eyes. She held herself solely responsible for what had happened to her sister. Her shame was clearly about the relationship with Aragon, but Sam wasn't going there. If he found out what the bastard had done to her, he probably *would* have to kill him.

He also saw dogged determination in her steadfast gaze, and that concerned him almost as much as the emotion. She wouldn't give up on this quest to rescue her sister, with or without his help. And if she tried to go it alone, she could easily put both of them in jeopardy.

"You're right," he said at last. "I am a federal agent."

She regarded him warily. "What kind? And why should I believe you now?"

It was tough not to smile. "I'm with the Treasury Department, and I'm investigating Jason Aragon and his club."

Sam needed her cooperation, and he was betting the truth would be the easiest way to get it. Clearly she wasn't going to be dismissed—or easily handled. And she had damn little fear of authority, which told him she was used to dealing with it in some way.

Allegra Danner. He was more than curious what a background check on her would reveal, but he would have to run it himself, and there wasn't time for that now.

"I knew it." The comforter lifted and fell with her shoulders. "I *knew* you were a good guy."

Sam wanted to roll his eyes. In less than an hour she'd accused him of everything from sexual perversions with duct tape to being a gangster out to gun down Jason Aragon. Yeah, sure, he was a good guy.

"Let's talk strategy," she said. "I need you to get me inside—and down to the lower level—but once we're there, I can point you in the direction of a certain top secret room. Deal?"

Sam gave a weary shake of his head. She'd just played her ace—and probably bet everything she had on it. God save him from desperate women. At least she wasn't vulnerable *and* desperate anymore. That was a step in the right direction. Maybe.

"Look," he said, "I already told you I'd search for your sister. You give me the club's layout, including the lower level and the *secret* room, and I'll find Vix—or Victoria, or whatever the hell her name is—*if* she's anywhere to be found. That's the only deal I'm making."

"Won't work."

She'd barely let him finish. There *was* no right direction with this woman.

"My sister would never trust you," she said. "She'd think you were working with Aragon. She might even blow your cover. You *need* me in there with you. Why can't you see that?"

"Because you're a rank amateur. If you were any good, you wouldn't be sitting here, half-naked, on my bed." *And making it hard to think about anything but the goose bumps on your long, sexy, icy-cold legs—and the fullness sizzling in my groin.*

Bottom line, Sam wanted her clothed. She was too distracting otherwise.

"Half-naked, maybe," she said, "but I had you pegged from the beginning, Mr. Treasury Agent. And you don't know my sister. She's very unpredictable."

"Why does *that* not surprise me? You do realize that you could be cooling your heels in a jail cell," he warned. *Best place for her. Let her torture the male guards.*

"Why? I haven't done anything wrong. I didn't break in. The door was open."

The air-conditioning kicked in again. The sound of it wooshing on and off was beginning to annoy Sam, but he operated best at near-Arctic temperatures, especially with fiery, vulnerable women around.

"You're interfering with an ongoing investigation," he told her. "That's a serious charge, and I can hold you indefinitely without booking you. Trust me, you don't want that."

She rose from the bed, clutching the comforter around her. "And you can trust *me* on this. My family is well-connected, and I have powerful friends in Washington. If you arrest me, if you detain me, or try to hinder me in any way, I promise I will be back on the street the same day, and I'll go straight to Aragon with this bargain: my sister for Sam Sinclair."

Sam opened his mouth to speak, but she waved him off.

"Are you willing to put your precious investigation on the line, *Mister* Sinclair? Or your life? Aragon is deadly when crossed. He wouldn't hesitate to have you killed."

Sam imagined Aragon had more effective ways of dealing with people than murder, but she might know more than he did. He went silent, calculating the odds of his investigation going up in smoke. He didn't like them.

"If you're going to blackmail my ass," he said at last, "you might as well call me Sam. And stop threatening to go to Aragon. We both know you're not doing that. It won't get you your sister, unless you're willing to trade places with her."

Her chin jutted. "I'd be willing if it would get her out of there."

"Well, I'm *not* willing. And *you're* not up for grabs."

She studied him, now avidly curious, and he realized he'd said too much. Revealed too much. It was frightening how naturally that had happened. Maybe it was time to get the hell out of this business.

"Okay, so…what now?" she said, apparently thinking he'd changed his mind about taking her.

Time to get serious, Sam realized. He unbuttoned the cuffs of his white dress shirt and rolled up the sleeves, his eyes fixed on her the entire time.

"I'm good at what I do, Ally. Barring something unforeseen, I'll have your sister out of there in twenty-four hours, and no one will even know she's gone."

He would have to be sure of that last thing. He didn't want Aragon's security swarming the place, looking for a missing woman.

"Twenty-four hours? And if you don't make that deadline you'll take me in with you, right?"

He barely hesitated. "Sure." There. Eminently reasonable. What more could she ask? Of course, he wasn't taking her in no matter what happened with her sister, but she didn't know that—and he had no problem justifying the hedge. There were people in this world who had to be protected from themselves. She now redefined that category for him.

She was quiet enough that Sam had to wonder if he'd actually gotten through to her. Clearly she would risk a lot to get her sister back, but she wasn't crazy. He didn't believe she would expose herself by ratting him out to Aragon. And maybe she'd realized that she would only get in the club his way, if she were to force herself on him.

Although, if she were to back him to the wall with her naked body and force him to endure the softness of her breasts and her thighs, and her hot-as-hell lips, she could get in his way just fine…but only for an hour or two.

Cease and desist, you dumb shit, he told himself. You're bringing this grief on yourself!

As if coming out of a trance, Ally bent down and snapped up her skirt. "I don't have twenty-four hours and neither does Vix. If you won't take me, I'll find someone who will."

If he wouldn't *take* her…why did she say things like that?

As Sam watched her snatch up her pantyhose and shoes and turn away, it occurred to him that he was going to be an eyewitness to a dressing ritual. Hers. He'd always thought he preferred watching women undress. Maybe not. He'd know shortly.

A nerve sparked hard in his groin, warning him.

He glared at the floor—and took the anger he felt at

himself out on her. Good guy he wasn't. "I'd accuse you of losing your mind," he said, "but I don't think you have one. You're not going in there. With me or without me. You're *not*."

She whirled on him. "And how will you stop me? With duct tape? Or a bullet? Because that's what it's going to take."

Sam shot back. "It doesn't concern you that you may get your sister killed if you blow this? Or yourself? Or hell, me?"

She knelt to pick up the rest of her clothes, cradling them in one arm and struggling to keep the comforter in place.

He couldn't let her leave. Even if she didn't go to Aragon, she might tell another club member about him, and that was just as dangerous. Unfortunately, *he'd* been bluffing about having her arrested. He could have her detained temporarily by the local feds, but then he'd have to explain his reason for being in New Orleans and investigating the club without their knowledge. At this stage of the game that wasn't even an option. He was undercover, and the local office knew nothing about this operation.

"I didn't come here to interfere with your investigation," she said. "But I won't let you interfere with mine, either."

She paused, as if carefully considering her next words. "I have information about the club that only an intimate of Aragon's would know. You'll never find what you're looking for without me."

If she were lying she was getting adept at hiding the signals. "How close were you and Aragon?" As much as he wanted to avoid the details of their relationship, he had to ask. If she actually knew the location of a secret room or secret files or secret anything, that might change things.

*Might.* Truth was, he didn't want her in the club under any circumstances, and for lots of reasons, some of which he wasn't anxious to examine.

"Jason kept me prisoner in the lower level during the renovations, and I know where the safe room is. There's also a place called the Vault that I think you'd find interesting. You haven't been to the lower level yet, have you?"

He hadn't, nor had anyone else from Treasury. Other attempts had been made in the past to infiltrate Aragon's operation, but only one had gained access to the lower level, and that was before Aragon renovated the area. There was no intelligence on that part of the club, which meant that Sam would be flying blind.

"It's a maze down there," she said. "I could never draw you the map you're talking about, but once I see the place, I'll be fine. That's how my mind works. I require visual cues."

"You're delirious. Get dressed." Sam spun on his heel and headed out the double doors and into the living room. He needed some space, some time to think. As he sat down on the sofa he realized his head was throbbing. Ally Danner was supposed to be his hostage, but somehow she'd trapped him, too. If he allowed her to leave, and she carried out even one of her threats, his investigation was over. There was also the issue of her personal safety. And if that wasn't enough, he had her sister to deal with.

Two choices came to mind, and both of them sucked. He could tie her up and stash her somewhere, literally hold her captive until he'd completed his mission—and perhaps found her sister. She wouldn't be in his way, but it was still incredibly risky. He would have to find the perfect place to leave her, and he had no one to guard her. If she got free, or was found, she would almost certainly blow his cover before he could do anything to stop her. Plus, he'd have to check on her, get food to her and try to keep her from doing something stupid, like hurting herself.

He could almost guarantee that she *would* hurt herself, given her track record. She was a risk taker, whether she knew it or not. Cautious women didn't stake themselves out in graveyards to spy on notorious men's clubs or break into the hotel rooms of strange males.

His only option was to put her on a short leash. As long as she was with him, he could keep an eye on her. That could give him more control, and it might be the only way to keep them both alive.

He sensed she was behind him, standing in the doorway.

"I'll find my own way out," she said.

He sat forward, glowering at the floor. "One night."

"What?"

"I said *one night*. I'll get you in the club, but it's a one-shot deal. If we don't find your sister, that's it. I'm done— and so are you."

"*Okaaay.* When do we go? And how will we pull it off? Am I going to be your girlfriend?"

"No girlfriend stuff. You can be my personal assistant."

He heard the comforter shifting against her body. She was dressed by now, right? Hell, he hoped so.

"A personal assistant is going to look suspicious, Sam. So would a secretary, or a wife, for that matter. Members either go stag or with a female companion. That's just how it works, as you already know."

Yeah, he knew. He ran both hands down his face. He'd been on the move nonstop since before dawn yesterday morning, and fatigue was setting in with a vengeance.

"So, that only leaves one option. I'll have to be your female companion." She sounded not just resigned to her fate, but totally matter-of-fact about it. "Arm candy, sex kitten, lollipop. Whatever you prefer to call it."

He swung around to look at her. "Lollipop?"

She was wrapped up to her neck in the comforter, but when she saw his abject disbelief, she stuck out her tongue at him.

"Yeah, lollipop," she said, fluttering her eyelashes. "Something sweet and sassy. Lickable."

Sam laughed out loud. "You? Lickable? You really *are* delirious." The hurt look that shadowed her expression told him he'd offended her.

"Hey, I didn't mean that in a bad way," he said. "Take it as a compliment. A lot of women would be thrilled to know they're not lollipop material."

She wasn't thrilled.

He sank down, collapsing on the sofa in defeat. He was done apologizing. Some women could play the sex kitten and some couldn't. Ally Danner fell into the second group. Exhibit A? Her one hundred percent cotton panties. They covered her belly button!

A pile of clothes landed on the cushion next to him. They were hers—and worse news, if that was possible— she was now standing at the other end of the sofa. He refused to look at her, but could still see her in his periphery. Lucky him.

"You don't think I'm up to it?" she said. "Not sexy enough?"

The comforter he'd given her was part of the pile. Did that mean she was standing there naked? All kinds of images darted through his head. Would she have goose bumps all over her nude body? He could only imagine what her breasts would look like, all chilly and puckered. And how about those pale, quivering thighs? She had to have an incredible figure. He'd seen enough of her to fill in the blanks. Great legs and trim, tapered ankles. He could just bet her ass was great, too.

If he was any kind of gentleman, he'd have to warm her up, right? He couldn't let her stand there, puckered and goose bumpy.

Sam swallowed a moan of frustration. He'd just figured it out. She was working for Aragon, and she'd been assigned to render Sam helpless by slowly driving him insane with male hormonal confusion. "That's not what I meant," he said. "I never said you weren't sexy enough."

"Yes, you did." Her reply was soft, but challenging. Almost an invitation, that voice. She was up to something.

"Well, you just watch," she said.

He wanted to cover his head. "I'm not watching. Do you *see* me watching?"

"Are you afraid of naked women?"

"Hell, no." He pivoted just in time to see her bow her head. Her long dark hair fell forward, concealing her face from view. Other than the bra she was clutching to her breasts, she was totally naked, just as he'd imagined. Well, worse than he'd imagined. The downy thatch between her legs looked just as soft and glossy as the hair on her head.

Sam's stomach muscles clenched. What kind of exhibition was this? He could sure as hell see her belly button *now*. How did she know he wouldn't haul her sweet butt onto the sofa and shag the damn daylights out of her? He was thinking about it. As God was his witness, he was.

She raised her head and tossed back her hair, allowing Sam to watch the transformation that was taking place. Obviously, some invisible vixen had taken possession of Allegra Danner. The woman he'd spent the last hour with was still evident, but *another* woman was in the room, too, who might even *want* him to drag her onto the sofa, which was exactly why he wasn't going to do it.

Look at her. With her head cocked just enough to be sexy, she traveled the length and breadth of his body with her gaze, lingering unabashedly in places that good girls weren't supposed to linger. The tip of her tongue darted over her lips to wet them, and she crossed her arms over her breasts, squishing them just enough to create one of the sexiest poses he'd ever seen.

A slight movement riveted his attention. He could hardly believe that he was watching her thumb flick lightly over her nipple, teasing it into a hard little bud that pressed against the cotton material of her bra.

It took Sam a moment to clear the buzz saw from his throat. "What do you think you're doing?"

"Oh, I don't know," she said sweetly as she came around the couch in his direction. Her steps were slow and seductive. "This, maybe?"

Not once did her gaze falter or drift from his body as she approached him. She held out her hand. He didn't take it, but that didn't faze her. She gripped his wrist and tugged, still holding the bra cups to her breasts. Of course, one of those pale beauties had popped out and was almost totally exposed, but he didn't have time to appreciate the wonder of that event. She was determined to get him to his feet, and he didn't resist her, but as he stood, it hit him that he should.

He really should.

She came close enough that he could feel the heat shimmering off her body. The look in her eyes went from seductive curiosity to flat-out smoldering desire, and Sam's groin began to smolder, too.

"You've made your point," he said, forcing harshness into his voice. "Let's give it a rest."

He scrutinized her expression for any sign of capitulation.

But Ally Danner had no intention of giving it a rest. Not tonight anyway. Only moments ago, as she had stood in the bedroom doorway, her intuition had told her it was now or never. She either proved herself or lost him for good. Although she hated giving him credit for anything at this particular moment, he did have a point. If she couldn't pass muster as a sex bomb here in private, she certainly wouldn't be able to do it at the club.

It seemed to be working. Sam's darkening eyes were telling her that he was riveted by her seduction attempt. There was no way to know what he was thinking, but she was fairly certain he wasn't mapping out his next move on Aragon. His thoughts were centered on her and her alone.

She was just as surprised by her boldness as he was. What was she doing with this man, and just as importantly, what was she doing *to* this man? Even with her shivering ice-cold flesh and everyday undies, she had completely captured his attention.

She was operating on instinct, but for her next move, she tried a ploy she'd seen in the movies. Just the thought of it made her smile as she rose on her tiptoes and leaned close enough to kiss him, then blew softly on his lips instead. Sam jerked back, but at the same time, he grasped her waist, as if he couldn't decide whether to push her away or pull her close.

That's when the ploy backfired. The poof of air Ally sent his way worked fine, but when she inhaled, she caught a whiff of something that triggered a powerful impulse. Cinnamon, of course, which brought an immediate flashback of Red Hots, and sweet illicit kisses.

She broke away from Sam with a dizzy shake of her head, but she was far from finished with him. "Maybe I'd better get dressed."

"*Maybe* you'd better get dressed?"

He sounded incredibly grouchy, but she took that as a good sign. More proof that she had him on the ropes. "You seemed to enjoy watching me strip," she said. "Let's see how you like watching me put my clothes back on."

He brushed the fly of his pants, making a quick adjustment as he sank to the couch. She couldn't tell if he were trying to avoid her or if he wanted a ringside seat, but if he had anything to say he kept it to himself, even as she cupped her nearly exposed breast in her hand.

She feathered her nipple with her thumb and when that got no reaction from him, she began to languidly circle it with the tip of her finger. A deep thrill startled her. She watched her own puckering flesh react to the sensuality of her touch, and she wished that he would. React.

Maybe she'd rendered him speechless?

Avoiding his gaze, she lowered her other hand to gently touch herself at the juncture of her legs. It was only a light stroke, but it was enough to create some sparks. Was any of this working? She hazarded a shy glance and saw the reaction she'd been wondering about. *Thank God.*

Sam had settled back against the sofa, his long legs stretched out in a relaxed pose that belied his body's tension. He had an enormous erection, and the way his hand rested on his thigh led Ally's gaze straight up his inseam and stopped it right at the wall that his crotch had become.

She tore her eyes away and glanced at his face.

Those dark, baby-you're-in-big-trouble eyes were filled with lust.

Something snagged in her throat as she tried to swallow. It was hard to believe she could elicit this kind of reaction without even touching him. She hadn't been accused of being a man magnet since she worked at the club, and then it had all felt fake. This was *supposed* to be fake, but it felt real.

She didn't dare look at him as the last piece of clothing dropped to the floor. Instead, exquisitely aware of her shivering state, she retrieved her pantyhose from the sofa cushion and sat on the edge of the coffee table, in plain view of her audience, of course. She began rolling the nylon in preparation for sliding her foot into it.

"You call that getting dressed?" he asked abruptly.

"Actually, I call it a reverse striptease." She wouldn't let herself smile, but she was rather pleased that she'd thought of it. His tense expression said that he wasn't. Not one little bit pleased. However, his pants suggested that he was loving every second of it. Quite the conflict brewing in our boy.

This would all go much better if she acted as if she were the only person in the room and stopped glancing at him every five seconds. Watching him turn into a human fertility statue was making her as crazy as he was. In fact, maybe she would pretend that sliding pantyhose up her leg was the most sensual act a woman could perform on herself.

Her breathing seemed to slow as she eased her toes into the leg and then bent to appraise the lines and contours of her instep and ankle.

She heard a clicking noise and wondered if perhaps Sam's tongue had stuck to the roof of his mouth.

Once she had both legs encased, she rose, and with her back to him, gently tugged and shimmied her way into the hose. Naturally, she played with the fit, adjusting the crotch so it cupped her evenly, and slipping her hand inside to align the darts and seams. Getting form-fitting pantyhose just right should have been an Olympic event, especially the way she did it.

This particular pair were nude to the waist, which was why she normally wore underwear with them. Otherwise, they were showgirl sexy—and reminded her a bit too much of her past. She'd worked in the club and knew how hot a woman had to be to pass muster. She would have preferred not knowing, but she didn't have that option, so she was making the best of it.

Her skirt was within easy reach. Reminding herself to take her time, she stepped into the black mini and tugged until she had it where it was supposed to be. She inched the zipper up, aware that Sam was still watching her.

Her bra was next. Inspired by movie scenes where the woman turns away from the man and gracefully fastens her bra behind her back, making him work for a glimpse of her curves, Ally did her best. Not exactly graceful, but she got the damn thing hooked after several tries, and she could hear Sam make another one of those dry, clicking sounds.

Time to face the music, she decided. Give him one last look before putting on her camisole. And check him out as well.

But all she could see was the tent his erection had made in his pants. And despite her fervent desire not to, she began wondering how it would look and feel in the flesh. *Ally, don't go there. Don't.*

Heat rushed into her cheeks. An Asian coworker she often lunched with at the Smithsonian had told her once that the ancients referred to the male sex organ as the Heavenly Dragon and female as the Golden Lotus.

Sam had some major dragon action going on. Heavenly, she wasn't so sure about. She could easily imagine it spitting fire, though. Her mind didn't seem to want to imagine anything else. What would it feel like if she dropped to her knees and unzipped him, freed him and cradled the fiery monster in her soft palms? Would it scorch her tender pink skin? Not to mention seeking sanctuary in her cave?

*Think you might be getting carried away, Ally?*

She slipped on the camisole and rose, aware that the strap was drifting off her shoulder. When she met Sam's gaze she saw that it was as pointed as her thoughts—if atmospheric energy could be created between two people then they were on the verge of some stormy weather. Sam rose, came toward her, looking like a man intent on making his move.

Her throat tightened, and she couldn't have spoken without sounding strained. One more step and he would be next to her. What did he have in mind, and would she go for it? She was crazy now, imagining how he might touch her, kiss her. Was that part of the bargain she had just struck with him?

Her answer was bells. *Trill trill trill.* Bells?

Sam heard them, too. The sudden peel of chimes stopped him in his tracks. He glared at the writing desk. The phone was ringing, and Ally was shocked at her reaction. More than anything else, she was disappointed.

She picked up her suit jacket and slipped it on as Sam went to the phone.

"Hello," he said into the receiver. "Oh, yes, Angelic. Apparently we were disconnected."

Ally stopped buttoning her suit jacket and looked over at Sam, who returned her gaze as he listened intently. It was Angelic from the club, but why would she wait so long to call back? Ally didn't like the sound of this.

"It may have been a bad connection," Sam said, apparently trying to explain away the hang-up, "or the phones here at the hotel, some computer mix-up. No need for concern. Thanks for checking, though."

He went silent again, listening. "No, really everything's fine. It's very kind of you to take such good care of your members. Actually I called you because I arrived at the hotel to find a visitor in my room—"

Ally's heart froze in her chest. Was he going to betray her?

"—and I was calling to see if you—"

He *was* going to betray her. He had Ally's real name. All he had to do was tell Angelic that one of Aragon's girls had broken into his room, and give Angelic her name. Ally's cover was blown. Now, Jason Aragon would have them both—her *and* her sister, and Sam was responsible.

Maybe he was in on it. Maybe he always had been.

Ally might as well be a dead woman.

# 7

SAM CONTINUED TO STARE at Ally as he spoke into the receiver. "I was calling to see if you could set up reservations for dinner," he said, finishing his sentence to Angelic.

Ally tried not to show her relief, but it was profound. Her legs were about to give out. Any minute she would have folded up like a deck chair.

"Who?" Sam paused for a mere second and then said, "It's my girlfriend. She's stopping over on her way to the east coast. We'd like to have dinner at the club tomorrow. Can that be arranged?"

She was in. Damn. Hot damn.

"Great, thanks. Seé you then." Sam hung up the receiver, saw Ally's expression and gave her a stern shake of his head. *Save your gratitude, he was telling her. And whatever you do, don't run over here and throw yourself in my arms. I'm not your savior. I didn't ask for any part of this.*

Still, Ally couldn't quite contain herself. "You're taking me? As a *girlfriend?*" She needed to hear him say it.

"I know it's a stretch," he said, his tone deadpan, "but if you say nothing and do nothing except gaze at me adoringly, maybe no one will notice that you're not a very good vixen."

This man had it coming. "Why do we have to wait until tomorrow night?" she asked. "Couldn't we go over there now? The club is open into the wee hours."

"Because your friend Jason isn't leaving until tomorrow and we can't risk running into him."

"Could we go for lunch? I want to get Vix out of there, Sam."

"No, *really?*" He shook his head. "I made the reservation for dinner and that's when we're going. I've never been to the club for lunch and it would draw attention if suddenly I changed my routine."

Ally reminded herself that Jason was probably using her sister as bait and was unlikely to hurt her. Their plan could wait until dinner. It would have to. "I just don't want to take any chances," she said.

"Neither do I." He zapped her with yet another stern look. "One rule and this is not negotiable. You stick to me like glue, understood? You do exactly as I say. No arguing, no fighting, no excuses. Once we're inside the club, it's my way or the deal's off."

"Of course." She wasn't going to fight with him now, although she wasn't entirely sure she would obey without question if and when the time came.

"Good." Sam's shoulders dropped, possibly with relief. He headed for the small minibar in the cabinet beneath the television. "I need water," he mumbled. "Do you want anything?"

Ally wrapped the comforter around her and shivered. Her clothes hardly made a difference. "No, thanks," she said, plunking down on the couch.

She watched him pull a bottled water from the minibar, unscrew the cap and drink straight from the bottle. Kind of sexy, actually. Like watching a world-class athlete quench his thirst. It emphasized the sensuality of Sam's profile, and especially his lips. They were full, and perpetually on the verge of a cynical twist.

When he was done drinking, he grazed his mouth with the back of his hand, perhaps to catch any runaway drops, and nodded with satisfaction. He didn't set the bottle down, but he did shift his body slightly, as if trying to readjust something below belt level.

That seemed to be his signature move, Ally thought wryly, wondering if he was unusually large in the relaxed state or just needed better-fitting underwear.

She could have used some underwear. Her nude pantyhose were a little moist in certain places. The reverse striptease had left her all steamed-up, even in this subzero clime. Interesting how seeing him get aroused had aroused her, even though her only goal had been to make him see that she could handle herself in the club.

She wasn't a very good vixen? He had a few things to learn.

She pushed the thought out of her mind, and brought up something that had been bothering her. "Does it seem odd to you that Angelic waited so long to call back?"

Sam nodded, as if he'd been thinking about the same thing. During the course of the evening, Ally had noticed that there was a certain look he assumed when he was in "reflective mode." His gaze turned inward and the furrow on the bridge of his nose deepened. Even his lips pursed slightly. On the other hand, when he moved into "investigative mode," his eyes took on a raptor's focus.

"Good question," he said softly.

Reflective mode. "Was Angelic suspicious?"

Sam screwed the cap on the bottle and put it back in the fridge. "Could be."

"Then why would she wait?" Ally said. "Why not call right back?"

"Also a good question. I think she may have been recording the call. Normally she has a slight Creole accent, but there was no sign of it during the call."

"She was disguising her voice?"

"No, she was enunciating. I think she wanted to be sure everything was picked up. People talk differently when they're using audio surveillance. They don't realize it, but they do."

"They're keeping tabs on you, Sam. I have to stay here tonight. I *can't* leave. If you're being watched, someone will see me."

Sam had already considered the possibility that he was under surveillance, and planned for it. But that was before his visitor showed up. He glanced over at her on the sofa, still wrapped in the throw. It pained him to concede that she might be right.

"Sam, did you hear me?"

"I heard you."

"Well?"

With the toneless resignation of a French Legionnaire facing a firing squad, he said, "Looks like I have a roommate."

As he studied the stork pattern in the Oriental carpet, avoiding what he imagined would be another bright smile, he found himself wondering what she wore to bed. Not that he planned on going to bed with her, but there was always the chance of an encounter late at night on the way to the bathroom. Hopefully it wouldn't bother her that he slept in the raw.

She began waving to get his attention. "Do you think the suite could be bugged?" She mouthed the words, as if that could possibly make any difference now. They'd been openly talking about phone tapping for the last ten minutes.

"I checked the rooms before I left," he said.

"Someone could have been in here while you were gone."

"Someone was—you."

Ally decided not to push it. Still she lowered her voice. "So, you were expecting surveillance," she said. "Is that why there's nothing personal in your suite?"

He nodded, stifling a yawn. "I'm bushed. I'll sleep on the sofa. You take the bed. We'll sort out the rest of this in the morning."

Ally considered vacating the sofa as he walked over and sprawled at the other end. His head dropped back on the pillows, and he closed his eyes, apparently serious about sleeping there. She allowed herself to observe him for a moment as she thought the situation through. The vague sense of familiarity still lingered, but he didn't look much like a ghost—tonight. He looked pretty scruffy, and even though she had to admit it was hugely appealing, his idea of sleeping arrangements wasn't going to work.

Moments later she'd come up with the only possible solution. She had another proposition for him, but it was for the sole purpose of assuring that she got into the club tomorrow. Vix was in that place, and Ally doubted that Jason was going to be gone for more than a couple days. This was Ally's one shot, and she didn't have much time.

"Can I say something?" She made her tone extrasolicitous. Based on their brief history, she was about to make a suggestion she knew he would hate. The man gave her a complex. Really.

He rolled his head toward her. "Like you need permission?"

"Sam, I've been mulling this, and I think we should sleep together. In the same bed, I mean."

"Excuse me?"

"If you're being watched it could be by someone on the hotel staff. Even the maids could be passing information on to Aragon or Angelic, on his behalf. If you're going to claim to have a girlfriend, you'd better have one."

Ally hadn't had all that much trouble finding a cooperative maid. Since the maid had taken a risk to help her, she'd decided not to mention it to Sam.

"Let's save the girlfriend act for the club," Sam said. "I haven't got the energy."

He closed his eyes.

Ally persisted. "Do you know how easy it is to bribe someone on the housekeeping staff for information? Even if we messed up the bed to make it look like we'd both slept there, the maids have keys. They can walk in at any time—and do. We can't take any chances, Sam. This is my sister's life at stake. And ours, too, if we're found out."

Apparently he had nothing to say about that. His eyes remained stubbornly closed, and either he was ignoring her, or he'd fallen asleep. She didn't know which was more aggravating.

Ally entertained the idea of pouring a bucket of water over his head, but the closest thing the suite offered was a chilled bottle from the minibar. Finally she got up from the couch and strode to the bedroom. Let him wake up with a crick in his neck. She would have the whole bed to herself.

"MOVE OVER SO I can get in there." The gruff male command carried across the shadowy darkness of the bedroom.

Ally lifted her head off the pillow, trying to locate the disembodied voice. "Sam?"

"Were you expecting someone else?"

"I wasn't expecting *you*," she said. "What happened to sleeping on the sofa? Get cold out there?"

She could see him now. A formidable figure came right up to her bedside and loomed over her in the moonlight.

"Are you moving or not?" he wanted to know.

"Why should I? Go around the other side."

He sighed like a man sorely tested. "I need to be on the side by the phone, in case it rings."

She rose up on her elbows and stared at him. "Now you *want* to sleep with me? Like you're insisting on it?"

He folded his arms over his chest. His bare chest, she realized as the light flickering over him gave glimpses of detail. A beautifully cut pectoral muscle and a rock-hard nipple. Would it be tawny, like the rest of him? Or a deeper richer sienna brown?

He really was serious about getting into bed with her—*and* he'd taken his clothes off. No way was she going to look down.

"I can hear voices in the hall," he said, "and it sounds like the hotel staff. It's keeping me awake."

"Poor baby. Why don't you just admit I was right about sleeping together? We can't take any chances, Sinclair."

"*Okay*, you were right. Now, move your sweet ass over, Danner, or I'll move it for you. Are you prepared to take *that* chance?"

She was. Lord only knew why, but she was. Within

seconds, she came to her senses, but she didn't scramble to get out of the big man's way, as he probably wanted her to. She took her sweet time moving her sweet ass. In fact, she dragged it an inch at a time across the hotel's thousand thread count sheets.

Once she was officially on the other side of the bed, she turned her back to him with a haughty sniff. *Totally disinterested, Sinclair. Get the message?* She was aware of every bounce of the mattress, every creak of the springs. It had been a long time since she'd been in bed with a man. She wasn't going to let herself think about how long, or she would start fantasizing about the thrill of hot, hard bodies coming together in the night, the rush of hearts and heavy sighs, and the rare pleasure of long, drawn-out soul kisses with someone whose touch you desperately craved.

She would start thinking about how hungry she was to be touched—and she couldn't let herself think about that. It hurt too much thinking about that.

It wouldn't be that way with him anyway, she reminded herself. He'd probably draw a line down the middle of the bed and tell her not to cross it. The man had some weird thing about women and sex. Women and love she could understand. But how many men drew the line at sex? She would have been questioning her attractiveness if he hadn't had erections every five minutes.

Her eyes snapped open as she felt a hand slide around her waist.

Suddenly she was being pulled backward with uncom-promising strength and speed. The sheets slipped through her fingers as he dragged her across the bed and up against the wall of his body. And there she was, her back pressed up against his front.

"What are you doing?" she squeaked.

"It was your idea that we sleep together, so let's do it right," he said. "If a maid sneaks in here, we'll be curled up like spoons. What could be more convincing?"

The hair on his thighs tickled the back of her legs, and her tailbone was nestled up against something soft. It could have been shorts. Or not. She ran her toes up his leg to his knee, and then she reached behind her and touched his hip with her hand. She patted around, but couldn't feel any clothing.

"Are you naked?"

"Where are you going?" he said as she wriggled away from him.

When he reached for her this time, he got a handful of shirt material. "What the hell are *you* wearing?" He tugged her toward him.

"One of your shirts. Armani, I think."

"Armani, lovely. Come here, dammit."

Ally smiled despite herself and eased back into the shelter of his body. The heat coming off him was miraculous, and unless she was mistaken, there was another miracle of nature going on. Her shirt—well, technically, it was his shirt—had hiked up in the back, and something that felt suspiciously like a lead pipe was nudging her exposed bottom.

Not shorts. Shorts stayed soft.

Sam Sinclair might not find her attractive, but the beast between his legs was nuts about her.

"Maybe we should do some moaning and thrashing," he whispered in her ear. "Just in case the room is bugged."

"Seriously?" She craned around to look at him. "Okay, let's do it."

He peered at her, disbelieving. "You really would do anything to get your sister out of there, wouldn't you."

Ally rolled over and scooched back into place, her bottom nestled against his hardening member. He had no idea.

HOW THE HELL had she managed to fall asleep?

Sam himself was wide awake—and had been all night. He was lying behind Ally, enduring the softness of her body. And she was snoring, too. Okay, technically, it probably wasn't snoring, but there was something slightly raspy and sexy about the way she breathed, and it was getting to him.

For one thing, it was keeping him awake. For another, it had him thinking about things that made his gut clench. Like mixing business and pleasure.

He'd made that mistake early on in his law enforcement career, when he was young and stupid. God—and what a hell of a mess he'd created. He'd been a rookie at the Treasury Department with just two years of service under his belt when his older partner had been killed, trying to apprehend the kingpin of a smuggling ring.

Ray Sayles had left a wife and a teenage girl, both of whom Sam adored. Sam had been single when he got the Treasury job, and the Sayles family had all but adopted him, inviting him for dinner and holidays. So when Ray died, Sam had fallen into the role of friend and protector.

But it hadn't been long before the gut-wrenching loss of Ray, coupled with the acute vulnerability of his widow, Linda, had changed the relationship into something else, and Sam hadn't had the life experience to handle it. Linda had turned to him for consolation, and when he'd held her, he'd felt consoled as well. One day, her pain apparently unbearable, she'd begun to pour her heart out to him, telling him how desperately lonely she was, and as Sam clumsily attempted to dry her tears, she'd kissed him.

He'd returned the kiss, but it was nothing more than a tender, caring gesture until some strange chemistry had ignited, perhaps born of loss and loneliness on both their parts. She'd clung to him, sobbing, and Sam had been astonished at his own need for solace. He'd managed to stop the embrace from turning into something else, but it had been excruciatingly awkward. The last thing he'd wanted was to embarrass her, and she had been even more bereft when he'd excused himself and left.

The next time it happened, neither of them had managed to stop.

They'd been two people trying to ease their grief. For a few moments they had been able to push away a terrible, unpredictable tragedy and cling to the hope that they could be whole again. Things like that happened when people stared into the eyes of death.

It had happened to Sam and a lovely woman who had just wanted not to hurt so much, even for a short time. But there had been no way to explain that to Ray's seventeen-year-old daughter when she'd walked into the bedroom and saw her mother in the arms of her father's partner.

Sam never again wanted to see that look of shock and horror on a child's face. He would rather have been the one who died.

He got out of their lives after that. The daughter had accused him of betraying all of them, even her dead father, and Sam knew he would be a constant reminder of her pain, of all their pain. He couldn't have defended himself, and she wouldn't have understood anyway. He didn't really understand it, either.

He had continued to help the family with money and support but never saw them again. And he never again confused the two roles in his life. He signed up to work undercover for a special unit in Treasury, and it soon became apparent that working undercover and normal life didn't mix. When what you did for a living involved changing identities and vanishing for varying periods of time, it was impossible to sustain a relationship. Even friendships were tough.

And maybe he'd unconsciously set it up that way. Distant enough so that he didn't get hurt anymore—or hurt anyone else.

It could get messy when you got too close. Like now.

He glanced down at the woman who was lying close enough to him to feel as if she were a part of his body. And wondered at his own sanity.

She was born to be a wicked little kitten with her wide dark eyes and plain cotton undies. He hoped she never figured it out.

The snowy-white pillowcase cradling her head brought out the contrast of her dark hair and luminous skin. He would have described her facial features as aquiline and classically European, even aristocratic. But there was nothing aristo-cratic about the firm, warm buttocks she'd pressed to his belly, or the way she kept breathing like an asthmatic kitten.

Why that should be sexy, he didn't know, but every-thing she did seemed to drive him nuts. His gut had turned itself into a clenched fist when he'd discovered that she was sleeping in his shirt. Probably, like most men, he was a possessive enough bastard to love the idea of a naked woman inhabiting his clothes. Call it pride of ownership— and he didn't mean the shirt.

Men. Neanderthals. All of 'em.

Poor jerks. No match for women whatsoever.

He didn't know whether to laugh or cry remembering her reverse striptease. His body hadn't known what to do, either. She'd turned his penis into a drawbridge, raising and lowering it with a bat of her lashes.

*Fatal Distraction.* Hollywood ought to make the movie. Even now, he should be focused on the Aragon case, but his mind didn't want to work with her next to him. It wanted to drift and play, which at the moment meant wondering what it would be like to slide his shirt off her shoulder and kiss the delicate skin.

He rolled back his head. Hell, Sam. Might as well fire up a blowtorch in a gunpowder factory. Even something as innocent as a kiss on the shoulder was dangerous. *Who should know that better than you?*

He had to get out of this bed.

It took the mental focus of a gymnast to ease his body away from hers without waking her. As he left the bedroom, he stole a last look at her and knew that making love to this woman would be the end of him, the end of life as he knew it.

In so many ways, she was everything he wanted, but couldn't have. He loved her spirit and her nerve. Nothing stopped the woman. She was probably braver than he was. Maybe that's what had him thinking so crazy—and it *was* crazy. She could never adjust to a life like his, nor should she have to.

There were lots of reasons to keep his distance. Stable relationships didn't run in his family, and so far, he hadn't shown any signs of breaking the mold. The various tragedies that had haunted his family made him wonder if the line could be cursed. Besides, he'd partnered up with Ally to get help with his mission. All she wanted in return was help with hers. When she found her sister, she would be out of his life forever. Why start something he couldn't finish?

All good reasons. Damn good ones.

But he still wanted to kiss her shoulder.

It startled him as he saw her reach behind her and touch the sheets, tugging on them as if she were searching for him in her sleep. His throat tightened, making it hard to swallow. He turned and left before the temptation to crawl back into bed with her got the better of him.

ALLY WOKE UP to the sound of grunts and groans coming from the other room. She rolled onto her back and stared up at the ceiling, listening. The last thing she remembered was a threesome right here in this bed—her, Sam and his lead pipe. She probably had a permanent indention back there.

But it was daylight now, and he was no longer in the bed with her.

The grunting got heavier, louder. Ally could hear strangled obscenities. It sounded like Sam had been ambushed. Was he fighting off an intruder?

She sprang out of bed and grabbed the table lamp from the bed stand, yanking the cord from the wall. The suite was still too cold to sustain human life, but there was no time to search for clothing. Sam's shirt would have to do. She pulled it down over her butt as she headed for the living room. But the sight that greeted her there stopped her dead in the doorway.

Sam was in the center of the Oriental rug, doing push-ups in his boxer shorts. Ally could hardly believe it. She had to think the lead pipe had something to do with his exertion, and she felt a little foolish with a lamp in her hand. Did men really do those things to combat sexual frustration?

She stood for a moment, unseen, and marveled at his physique. Maybe this was a bona fide workout routine. He must work out *a lot,* she thought. The major muscle groups rippled along the surface of his body like rivers, and yet they looked as solid as iron bands. Amazing.

But perhaps a little too physical for this time of the morning?

She hadn't even had a cup of coffee yet. He looked up as she cleared her throat. "I thought you were being attacked," she said.

"Was I that loud?" He finished the last of his push-ups. "Damn it's hot in here."

"Hot? Do you see this?" She waved her hand in front of her face.

He fell back on his haunches, breathing heavily. "No…what?"

"It's my breath, Sam. I can see my breath coming out of my mouth!"

A husky sound forced out of him as he pushed to his feet. It sounded almost like laughter. "I don't like being too comfortable," he said. "It diminishes my concentration. Make me feel dull."

"Fine, but I'd like to feel my fingers and toes! Can't we crank it up about forty degrees, at least?"

He mopped his face with a hand towel, then went over to the thermostat and turned off the air-conditioning. "Better?"

"Yes. Thank you." His body glistened with beads of sweat. God, he was sexy standing there, just smiling. Maybe that last part bothered her most. Right now he looked very much like a man she would love to have a relationship with: big, strong, handsome, and a sense of humor. Of course, it was all an illusion. He must have gotten up early, gone out and killed somebody. That's why he was smiling.

"How about a shower?" she suggested. Her voice wasn't as crisp as it was just a moment ago.

"Is that an offer? More boyfriend-girlfriend stuff? Or are we conserving water now?"

"We're getting clean," she said. "You're sweaty and stinky."

"And your point?"

*Another smile? Yes, he must have killed someone. Definitely.*

"Order some coffee," he said. "When I get back I'll tell you my plans for us today."

He swept past her into the bedroom, leaving Ally to wonder what he meant by plans. Sam had his reflect and investigate mode—and she had her decipher mode, which was imperative when dealing with a cryptic law enforcement type. She ordered the coffee and quickly cleaned up the suite, all the while trying to puzzle out his intent, but as she dropped his empty water bottles into the wastebasket, she noticed a folded piece of paper near the living room's front door.

Someone had slipped a handwritten note under the door.

# 8

SAM'S LEGS were almost too long to fit in the low-slung Porsche Targa, Ally couldn't help but notice as he folded himself into the driver's seat, keyed the engine to a low roar and put the powerful car in gear.

She breathed a sigh of relief as they drove away from the hotel.

He still hadn't told her about his plans for the day, but she had a surprise for him, too. The note she'd found slipped under the door was in her purse where she'd stashed it until they were safely away from the hotel. She wasn't sure what Sam would do when she read it to him, so she wasn't taking any chances.

He glanced her way, possibly because she'd been staring at his legs. She didn't offer to explain that lots of women found long legs on men to be every bit as visually stimulating as their legendary rear ends. And if they were wearing tight blue jeans and a black V-necked pullover like Sam's, you could appreciate both.

"What's wrong?" she said, aware that he was frowning at her outfit. She had on the same suit she'd been wearing yesterday. It was a little worse for the wear, but not as bad as all that.

"Not sexy enough," he said. "If you're going to be my girlfriend, you need to look the part."

"What? You want me to dress like a hooker on Bourbon Street?"

His mouth curved into a grin. "Now, you're talking."

"This is the sexiest thing I brought with me," she said, brushing at the wrinkles in her skirt.

"Which is exactly why I'm taking you shopping."

"Shopping? Now?"

He nodded. "That's the plan for today. The hotel concierge suggested we try the shops on Canal Place. She mentioned Saks and Ann Taylor."

Ally knew the area. Definitely upscale, and they weren't far away, but she had a better idea. "There are some great little shops in the Garden district. One of my favorite boutiques is there."

That got her a suspicious look from Sam. "Am I going to like this place?" he asked.

"Are you kidding? If you want sexy, you'll *love* this place."

Ally had to laugh at his skeptical expression. She gave him directions, and he turned his attention back to the road. This was her opportunity, she realized.

"Sam, remember I told you that the hotel staff is easily bribed? Well, I happen to know that because in a way, I bribed one of them."

"In a way?" He pulled into the left lane and made a turn. "Are we talking about the woman who let you into my room last night?"

"We are." Not much point denying it, she reasoned. Any good investigator would have seen the connection. "This morning she slipped this note under the door warning me that someone's been asking about you."

Ally took the note from her bag and read the scribbled sentences aloud while Sam drove.

"'Are you all right, ma'am? If you're still there with Mr. Sinclair, I want you to know that last night a man tried to pay my friend Raoul for information about Mr. Sinclair's comings and goings. Raoul is a security guard at the hotel. He didn't tell the man anything and neither did I.'"

Sam took the note, glancing at it as he drove. "How well do you know this woman?"

"I met her for the first time when I was scouting the hotel, trying to figure out how to get into your room. I told her about my sister, hoping she'd help me. She told me she'd grown up in Guatemala and her sister had been kidnapped and killed by rebels there. She broke down and cried."

"Do you trust her?"

"You're going to think I'm crazy, but I felt a bond with her, and I think she did with me. Otherwise, why would she risk putting a signed note under your door to warn me? She didn't even know for sure that I was there."

"I'd like to hang on to this." Sam tucked the note in his jeans pocket. "It's important that we go shopping just as we planned, but when we get back to the suite, I want you to fix the two of us drinks and chitchat about our shopping trip, the weather—whatever, just act nonchalant as I wander around the place and check it out."

"You think we're under surveillance?"

"If we're not already, we will be."

"Okay," she said, aware that the mood in the car had abruptly changed. He was back in investigative mode, and she almost wished she hadn't had to tell him about the note. She'd been enjoying the lower-key Sam.

Now that he was deep in thought, Ally hoped he

wouldn't come to the conclusion that it was too danger-ous to take her into the club. If Aragon had men skulking around the hotel, he was either already suspicious of Sam or he routinely went to such extremes to check out platinum key members.

Probably the latter, Ally decided. His possessiveness and need to be in control were a large part of what had driven her away. She didn't doubt he was paranoid as well. His Platinum Inner Circle key was something he'd kept totally under wraps, and she had no idea how the security was handled.

"Could this man be working for anyone other than Jason?" Ally asked, trying to draw Sam back into conver-sation. "Perhaps another case you're working on?"

"I'm not working on any other cases. This one is my sole priority."

With that he let silence settle around them again, and Ally didn't have the nerve to breach it.

She could see by the narrow, tree-lined streets that they were coming up on the area she'd told him about. "Left up here," she told Sam, and almost as soon as he turned, she spotted the shop, tucked in the middle of a row of small, artsy boutiques.

"There it is," she said, pointing to the quaint cottage-like storefront. "Pull over and park. There's a spot in front."

Sam parked the Porsche at the curb, and Ally was letting herself out when he appeared and offered his hand.

"I'm the gentleman gambler, remember," he said, helping her out of the car and onto the brick-lined walkway.

"Yes, sir," Ally replied. She was nearly enfolded in his arms as he reached around behind her to shut the car door.

She could smell the cinnamon on his breath and feel the warmth of his body heat. She quelled the urge to move away, aware that she rather liked the feeling of security his closeness gave her. He had a way of making her feel protected even when he was being annoying about it.

He was staring at her, she realized, waiting for her. For a second, she felt flustered.

"I've always loved this place," she said, drawing away from him with some effort.

She indicated the shop's shuttered windows and wrought-iron accents as they walked toward it. Red geraniums hung on the porchlike facade of a charming clapboard cottage, tucked away behind a blooming hedgerow.

Sam stopped dead in his tracks as he noticed the signage. "Sassy Ass! You've got to be kidding me. Who names a shop Sassy Ass?"

"A smart retailer, that's who. This is New Orleans. And, by the way, I'm paying for all of this. I insist."

"Insist all you want, but you're not paying. You can't be a kept woman unless you're actually being kept, can you? If someone is tailing us, he's sure to ask a few questions of the shop clerk after we leave, and how would it look if the clerk revealed that the lady had paid the bill. Our cover would be blown."

Ally couldn't argue with that. Nevertheless, she felt the need to warn him. "This kind of clothing can be expensive. More than you can probably imagine."

Sam snagged her arm and brought her to a halt. "Don't worry about the money. I have plenty, and if I drop a few thousand on clothes, I'll get it back at the tables tonight."

Ally glanced pointedly at his hand on her arm, establishing a psychological boundary, even if she couldn't establish a physical one. "Are you really a gambler or is that just a part of your cover story?"

He shrugged. "I've raked in a few pots." He caught her around the waist, pulling her close as he opened the shop door. "Behave yourself," he whispered in her ear, letting her know what he thought of her *boundaries*. "Think docile and adoring."

THE DRESS was a hot little number. The supershort skirt was made up of tiers of champagne pink ruffles that curved subtly up to a bodice as flouncy and feminine as the skirt. The one remarkable distraction from all the cascading chiffon was a neckline that dropped all the way to Ally's breastbone. The plunge was breathtaking, as was the blushing skin it revealed.

Ally's breasts had never looked more full and touchable. Her legs were as long and supple as a model's. But staring at her reflection in the mirror made her acutely uncomfortable.

The dress took her back to a time when *she* had been the hot little number. It had been part of the job description if you were Jason Aragon's woman, and she'd been happy to oblige. She'd briefly loved all the attention, but she hadn't loved what came with it. He'd been a perfect gentleman at first, showering her with gifts and attending to her every need. But Jason was dominant and territorial, and not long into the relationship he'd begun to question her whereabouts when she left the club. When she'd discovered he was having her followed, she'd threatened to leave. He'd retaliated by confining her to a room on the lower level until she came "to her senses." That was how Ally had become intimately familiar with the area.

She'd managed to jam the door lock in a way that went undetected, which freed her to roam the lower level while it was under construction. She had made several attempts to escape, but hadn't succeeded until the night of the club's Mardi Gras masquerade ball when she had dressed up as a court jester. Covered from head to toe in spandex and sequins, she'd walked out the front door in plain view of everyone.

It seemed Jason still hadn't forgiven her for that.

"Everything okay in there?" Sam called to her.

He was waiting just outside the luxuriously appointed private dressing room where the store manager had brought them after Sam explained what he was looking for. If the manager had closed down the entire store for them, Ally would not have been surprised. When a customer let it be known that money was no object, things happened.

"I'll be right out." She touched the low-cut bodice, aware of her own glowing, tingling skin. The dress had worked miracles on her figure, but it was mostly illusion, unfortunately. Her legs were not *that* long, or her breasts that voluptuous. Amazing what a great cut could do. This one was so revealing Ally'd had to remove her underwear. All of it.

Showtime, she told herself. Her heart pounding, she spun around on bare feet and opened the velvet curtains. Chiffon floated over her naked skin like clouds as she entered the sitting area.

Sam was just waving off a proffered glass of champagne. One of the clerks had brought in a tray of luscious-looking goodies and left it on the coffee table in front of the divan where Sam sat.

He really was in his element, Ally realized. Women hovering and fussing over him, anxious to get his approval, which Sam wasn't giving them, of course. They didn't realize it took an Act of Congress to make the guy smile.

No one even noticed Ally, so she took the opportunity to check out how the shop's decor had dramatically changed. Seven years ago it had been starkly modern with neon art and track lights. Now it resembled the salon of a very upscale bordello. The clothes were still sexy and designer-priced, but the atmosphere was more sophisticated and elegant.

The clerks finished up with their tasks, leaving the store manager to prioritize the outfits she brought in order of Sam's preference. Once Sam had made his choices, he looked over and spotted Ally. His expression changed the moment he saw her. He sat forward on the divan, his focus narrowing, tightening on her with undisguised male interest.

"Do you like it?" she asked.

"Hell, yes."

"Oh, it's lovely!" the store manager burbled. "You're just lovely, my dear. It's perfect for you. And I have some—"

Sam cut the manager a look that said *enough already.* To her credit she got the message. "Why don't I give you two some privacy?"

"That would be nice." Sam was polite, but pointed.

As the manager left, Sam rose from the divan, his gaze roaming all over Ally, devouring her in a way that made her feel almost light-headed.

"Let's see the rest of you." He led her away from the

velvet curtain so that he could circle her and view the dress from all angles.

Could he tell that she had nothing on underneath? The skirt was lined with silk, but her pulse danced as he lingered behind her. What was he looking at back there? She could feel the heat of his gaze running up the back of her thighs and fanning over her derriere.

"What do you think?" she asked. "Shall we get this one?"

His eyes were dark and smoky with sensual appreciation. Still he stepped back as if the question needed further consideration. "It's cute as hell, but you look like a birthday cake with too much frosting."

Heat singed Ally's cheeks. "Cute? This dress is killer. It wouldn't just stop traffic, it would cause a pileup."

But Sam was already across the room and was going through the rack of clothes. The manager had taken the two or three outfits he liked best and hung them at the front of the rack. He pulled one out and held it up.

"Let's try this," he said. "I want to see less frosting and more of you."

She peered at the swatch of lace fabric, but there was so little of it she couldn't tell what it was. It resembled pearlescent tubing with sleeves. She could see possibilities for venting a dryer, but not clothing.

"Whatever you say." *How's that for docile?* She graced him with a smile and disappeared behind the curtain, not wanting him to know that she was sharply disappointed by his reaction to her pink champagne ruffles.

She wasn't thrilled with his replacement, either. The dress, or whatever it was, had more spandex than material, she realized as she wriggled and scooched her way into it. The fabric was a delicate pearlescent mesh and had enough clinging power to be a second skin. It was plentifully adorned with clusters of flowers, but the flesh-colored spaces between the clusters *were* Ally's flesh.

It was easier getting the dress off than on. There was something she wanted Sam to see, but it wasn't a lace tube dress. She had another little surprise in store.

"TA-DAH." She stepped through the open curtain and did a little pirouette, waiting for Sam's reaction. "What's wrong?" she asked.

His expression was slightly incredulous. As corny as it sounded, he looked as if he'd seen a ghost.

"Sam? You don't like it?"

"What is it?" he asked, his voice oddly soft.

"A nightgown, I think." She turned again in the sheer white empire gown, hoping he'd see the subtle beauty of it. She'd picked up several things to try while they were browsing in the shop, and even though she'd known the nightgown wasn't the look they were going for, something about it had struck her as breathtaking.

The delicate white satin roses on the bodice and straps were the finest workmanship she'd ever seen, and the gown's empire lines lifted her breasts and gave her torso the length and grace of a ballerina's. She'd been born a princess, but she'd honestly never felt like one in her whole life. She knew that she would in this gown.

Clearly, though, it didn't work for Sam.

"How did you happen to pick that gown?" he asked.

"I don't know." She turned again. It was odd how the layers of silk made her want to twirl. "I just thought it was beautiful."

Sam was still watching her with something near suspicion in his gaze. "Apparently you've seen the portrait in the master bedroom."

She couldn't imagine what was wrong with him. "What portrait? What bedroom, for that matter?"

"The bedroom in the east wing at the club. The one that's supposed to be haunted. There's a portrait of a woman on the wall above the fireplace. She's wearing a gown like that."

"Really?" Ally glanced down, startled. She still wasn't certain what he was talking about. "Do you mean The White Rose? There's a picture of her in the master bedroom?"

"Yes, have you seen it?"

"No, never. That bedroom wasn't considered structurally safe. Several workmen were hurt there when the house was being renovated. Rumors started circulating that Rose didn't want them to touch the room she shared with Micha."

"No one *has* touched it," he said. "Angelic told me it was off-limits, but I decided to check it out anyway."

"Did you see any ghosts?" She smiled, hoping to lighten things up a little. He seemed to have gone into his reflective mode, almost to have disappeared in it.

"What I saw was eerie," he said, "as if someone had frozen time. Everything in the room is exactly as they left it a hundred years ago."

She really didn't know what to say. He was still looking at her as if he didn't know her, as if she were someone else.

"Is that bedroom the secret room you were talking about?" he asked her.

"No, of course not. There are two rooms, and they're both on the lower level. One is a safe room, where I believe

Vix is being kept. The other is Jason's brainchild. It's called the Vault, and it houses his computer system."

Finally she had his attention again. Sam was a man who played the odds, and the odds the Vault had the evidence he sought against Jason were good. She could almost see his mind working on how to obtain that evidence. But he wouldn't be able to do it in the time they had, not without her. She really did have something he needed.

"The gown is beautiful," he said. "Let's take it, along with whatever else you'll need."

"Shoes and accessories," she reminded him as she ducked back behind the velvet curtain.

"And a feathered mask or two," he added.

Ally heard him, but she was staring at her reflection in the mirror. Now she knew why Sam was startled. She did look different in some way that was hard to put into words. In the diffused light of the changing room, the image reflected in the mirror appeared almost ethereal. Ally hadn't seen the picture he talked about, but it felt as if she could have been looking at someone else, even a woman from another century.

She shivered, wondering if she'd imagined a chill in the air. The idea of Sam's having seen a ghost didn't seem quite so far-fetched now.

"I JUST LOVE all my beautiful presents, Sammy. How can I ever thank you!" Ally even managed to giggle as she made a fuss over the packages that Sam had piled on the dining room table.

She felt downright silly, but in the car on the way back from the boutique, he'd been emphatic about making idle chitchat when they got back to the suite. The Sam she knew—and didn't love—was back. He'd also told her once again to act docile and adoring—and she was going to do all of that, even if it drove him nuts. Sometimes the perfect punishment was getting exactly what you asked for.

"Glad you like them," Sam said tonelessly as he wandered around the room, scanning the baseboard, the walls, the ceilings. He stopped at the phone on the writing desk, picked up the receiver and touched the message button without actually depressing it.

Ally noticed that he casually tapped on the plastic case as he held the phone to his ear.

"Nothing important," he said, apparently referring to the messages. He returned the phone to its cradle and scanned the desk. Then, he sat down on the living room sofa, picked up a magazine and switched the table lamp on and off. "That's strange," he said, examining the lamp. "This one doesn't seem to be working. Let's try the other one."

Ally had no idea what kind of surveillance they might be dealing with, so she made it a point not to watch too closely as he continued to scope the place out. She pretended to be absorbed with her packages.

"I think I love this one best, Sammy," she said, making simpering sounds as she took the lace tube dress from one of the bags. "Maybe I'll wear it tonight."

"Maybe you won't," he said, a warning in his voice. "I'll be fighting off men all night if you wear that thing."

"But you picked the dress." She pretended to pout.

"To wear for me and me alone."

"I'll be good, especially to my Lion King."

He glanced back at her coquettish smile and made a

growling sound as he left the living room and entered the master bedroom. "I'm going to change into something comfortable," he called back.

"Great! I'll order us some food from room service. I'm famished." They hadn't taken time for breakfast or lunch, and she *was* hungry. She imagined he must be, too.

She was on the phone a moment later, ordering room service when she heard Sam call her name. There was something different about his voice—a low urgency that made her quickly finish the order and hang up the phone. When she walked into the bedroom, he was standing by the bed, unbuttoning his shirt, and his expression had a strange, thrilling intensity about it.

"Sam?" she said, her voice catching.

Just the sight of him made her thoughts go fuzzy. She assumed that he'd found a bug and was letting her know, but surveillance seemed to be the last thing on his mind.

"Are you all right?" she asked.

"I am now."

His shirt fell open and he reached down for his belt buckle. Ally almost turned and ran out of the room. Possibly she'd already driven him nuts?

"Come here," he said.

"Me?"

"Of course, you."

"Why?"

"Because I'm hungry as a lion…and I haven't eaten my fill today."

He had to be kidding. She peered at him, confused. He didn't look as if he were kidding. He looked like a big, hungry cat. His nostrils flared as he exhaled, and his incisors gleamed when he smiled.

"I don't want to be eaten," she said softly.

"Oh, yes, you do."

She was caught by the mesmerizing grip in his voice, and more than that, there was something utterly commanding in his gaze. His eyes burned with some kind of imperative need, and he was not going to be denied. Ally could hardly catch her breath, feeling as if she were being dragged over to him.

*"Ally. Come. Here."*

His voice was barely audible. Her heart was pounding so hard she felt almost ill, but she began to walk toward him. She didn't seem to have any choice.

When she was within his reach, he cupped the back of her head with his hand and pulled her close enough to kiss her. He wasn't rough, but he was insistent. He wasn't going to take no for an answer, and he probably wouldn't have stopped if she'd said the word.

"Don't argue, just kiss me," he whispered against her mouth.

His lips hovered, touching hers. It was a thrilling electrical sensation. Ally sighed, despite herself, and they embraced as if they were lovers. She laced her hands around his neck. Their mouths melted in a deep kiss, an astonishing kiss. His thighs came up against hers. Their bellies touched and her breasts softened, fanning against his chest.

The kiss deepened until she was swirling, confused, and then suddenly he was lifting her off her feet. Her breath came out in a surprised gasp as he pulled her down on the bed with him.

"I need to be inside you," he said. He caught her face with his hands, breathed the shocking words against her mouth. "I need that."

They rolled until she was on her back, and he was above her. "What in the world is going on?" she whispered, staring up at him.

He moved off her and glanced up at the smoke detector on the ceiling above them. He didn't have to say a word. Ally knew immediately that there was either a bug or a surveillance camera inside.

# 9

ALLY DRAGGED Sam back down to her, as if to kiss him. Instead she brushed her mouth against his, whispering, "Can't you disable it, baby?"

"It's a camera, *lollipop.* They'll see me doing it. We're being watched."

"Maybe we should have sex to keep them happy." She flashed him a sultry smile, wondering what had gotten into her. Normally she didn't find desperation sexy, especially her own desperation, but even that worked with Sam. Everything worked with Sam, and that concerned her. This wasn't just about her need to save her sister. She had a connection with him that couldn't be explained by any gratitude she was feeling for his help.

Still she had to remember that he wasn't helping her out of the goodness of his heart. He had his own agenda. And what if he decided to take her up on these challenges of hers?

He smoothed back her flyaway hair and got very, very close, continuing to whisper. "What's it going to take to make *you* happy?"

"Find my sister." *Right answer, Ally. Good girl.*

"Exactly—and how are we going to do that?"

"By convincing them that we're—"

"That we're what?"

Ally found it hard to breathe. "Lovers?"

He was using his thumb pad to smooth her hair—and staring down at her as if he could do sexual things to her with his eyes alone. That thumb of his could be a secret weapon, she acknowledged, recalling the feel of it on her breast. Apparently she'd answered correctly. She could see the darkness rising in his eyes like an erotic tide.

"Touch me like you want me," he said.

Ally kissed her fingers and touched them to his lips. It was the first thing that came to her mind. His answering kiss sent thrills spiraling through her. His mouth was velvety hot. She trailed her hand over his chest and down the muscular flatness of his belly. Suddenly she was pressing her palm to the fly of his pants.

The bulge she felt. It sent hot sparks up her arm.

"I want you," she told him. "I need you…inside me."

His eyes closed briefly. From pleasure?

Emboldened, she squeezed and felt him shudder under her hand. His body pulsed, responding uncontrollably to the gentle massage. The bulge got as hot as fire and hardened like stone. Seeing something like that happen was one thing. Feeling it was another.

"I need you inside me," she whispered again, meaning it this time.

Sam ground out a swear word, muttering something she didn't understand. That he wasn't a drawbridge? What was that supposed to mean?

There was no chance to ask. His fingers tipped up her chin, and his gaze held her. *Amazing.* For a moment she couldn't feel anything else. She couldn't draw breath. But then suddenly she had a whole lot more man—and pulsing muscle—than she knew what to do with.

"That was very convincing," Sam rasped. He seemed barely able to talk, which Ally took as a good sign.

"Are you trying to drive me nuts?" he whispered.

"Isn't that the idea?"

"No, *this* is the idea." He kissed his fingertips and brushed them over her lips, just as she'd done to him, but there was nothing tender about his gesture. It was hot and dark with his need to claim her. The dangerous glint in his eyes radiated his sexual hunger.

At the same time she realized he was protecting her, hiding her from view with his own body. No surveillance device could see her, but surely it could hear her! She couldn't suppress the husky sound that slipped out as his fingers moved down the curve of her neck and into the hollow of her throat, swirling lightly—and he watched her intently.

He wanted a reaction—and she didn't have the will to hold back. There was a part of her that didn't want to give him the satisfaction of even a sigh, but that would mean denying herself as well, which made zero sense at the moment. At least that was the argument her overwrought body was making.

His focus narrowed as he took in her excited state. He could have been an art connoisseur, appreciating a rare sculpture, feature by feature. Ally could feel the caress of his eyes as if they were his fingertips, and her flesh tingled with anticipation. Her breasts were tingly and tight. Her legs ached for some crazy reason.

He drew the camisole straps off her shoulders, both of them at once, and she swallowed back a cry of surprise. Was he going to bare her breasts? When he did, grazing her nipples with his thumbs, she heard herself whimpering.

There was as much reverence as lust in his eyes, and she didn't know which thrilled her most. Her whole body shook, but she didn't attempt to cover herself or do anything except allow him to undress her and admire her as though they were already lovers. She couldn't do anything else, but it had nothing to do with the camera, which couldn't see her anyway. Sam was still totally blocking the view.

She wanted him to undress her.

To slowly strip her naked.

Her entire body ached. But after he'd looked his fill, he drew the straps back up, and Ally thought she might die of frustration. She tried not to squirm and totally give herself away, but a moan slipped out.

Her nipples popped like pearls beneath the silk camisole, and the moment he spotted them, his eyes lit and he began to play, caressing them with his thumb and forefinger.

Finally Ally could stand it no longer. She caught hold of his hand and brought it to her mouth, swallowing the tip of his middle finger to the knuckle. She sucked and nibbled and stared him straight in the eye as she bit down on the fleshy pad. And he stared right back, as aroused as she was.

The knowledge sent pleasure flooding through her.

"Enough playing," she warned under her breath, "let's turn out the lights and get serious."

"I'm very serious," he said as he bent to her mouth. But all he did was tease her poor lips, nibbling on them as he lightly stroked her breast through the silk fabric.

The stimulation was too much. Ally wanted to be kissed thoroughly. Stroked thoroughly. She wasn't getting enough—of anything.

She drew open his shirt, entranced by the golden hair

that swirled over his pecs and lay flat against the muscles of his belly. She'd never seen such male sexual beauty. It was enough to make her ache for sex. The real thing.

Just the thought robbed her of reason. But not because she didn't want to. She didn't even care about the camera above them. There was a remote on the nightstand that controlled the lighting. They could turn off the lights, close the curtains and cover themselves with the comforter. If Sam had a weapon other than the one in his pants, he could shoot the smoke detector out of the sky. She didn't care about any of that. It was simply the shock of admitting she wanted it. With him. And how much.

"Make love to me," she said. "I mean it, Sam."

He hesitated, as if he'd heard the change in her voice.

"You don't believe me?" she whispered. She rose up and pushed him down, rolling on top of him before he could stop her. He did manage to block her leg as she threw it over him. He didn't seem to want her straddling him. In an astonishing show of physical power, he lifted her up and rolled her over, pressing her to the bed with his body.

"We'll do it when I say, lollipop."

He was trying to put her off, but Ally wasn't going to be put off anymore. She'd waited too long to feel this way. And honestly, she'd never felt this way in her life. It was exhilarating and liberating to want a man this much. She loved the spikes of desire coursing through her body.

She reached down and cupped him with her hand. "What do you say to that?" she whispered.

He groaned, and she felt the sounds echo deep inside her.

He looked down at her, his eyes lit with fire.

"Oh, you want it," she whispered. "You want it bad."

He kissed her and then he reached for the remote to turn out the lights. He'd just hit the button when the doorbell rang. Sam sprang up, looking as if he might go for a concealed weapon and blast somebody. As always, his hand grazed the crotch of his pants, seeking to bring some order, and this time, Ally knew exactly what he had to contend with down there.

"Oh, my God, it's room service," she said, just realizing it herself. "I ordered us a late lunch."

She sat up, trying to straighten herself. Her suit was already hopelessly mussed, and the way it looked now, she might as well throw it away. Her head was buzzing, but if she were certain of anything, it was that whoever had them under surveillance couldn't possibly have any doubts about Sam Sinclair and Ally Danner now. If they weren't lovers, they should be.

"BE CAREFUL IN THERE, Mr. Sinclair," the club's female security guard said in one of the huskiest, most sensual voices Ally had ever heard. "The ghosts are howling tonight."

"Is that right, Tanya?" Sam tucked a fifty-dollar bill in the woman's ammo belt as casually as if he routinely tipped that amount. "More icy cold drafts and slammed doors?"

Tanya's smile was a bit too eager. "One of our members tripped and fell down the stairs. Now you *know* that wasn't an accident. He didn't hurt himself, but he could have. The White Rose is on the prowl tonight. No man is safe."

"I'll be careful," Sam assured her.

Sam and Ally had stopped in the club's octagonal anteroom so that Ally could be patted down, which

Tanya was doing even as she carried on her conversation with Sam.

Sam had warned Ally that she might be searched when they arrived at the club. Sam had been spared the pat down because of his platinum key club status, but Ally wouldn't have been surprised if he'd had some regrets about that. Tanya had Wonder Woman's bullet breasts overflowing her camouflage bustier, and there was no way to describe her except ravishing.

"I hope it wasn't Mr. Aragon who fell," Ally said in a sweet voice.

With a tilt of his head, Sam warned her to be careful. She gave him an answering tilt, aware that the balance of power had subtly shifted between them. This was a public place, and he couldn't back her into corners and demand that she follow orders here. He didn't want to be discovered any more than she did. And even though he'd told her what his mission was, she'd begun to think he might have more at stake than he was admitting.

He really hadn't had to take her into this club with him. No doubt it was against Treasury procedure, and considering that she'd been tailing him and essentially broken into his room, she was lucky not to be in jail. But he hadn't reported her—and here she was involved in a dangerous scheme to find her sister. She couldn't help but wonder if he might have another agenda.

Tanya finished the pat down and handed Ally over to Sam, who'd been watching with interest. She hadn't missed Tanya's interest in him. Her dark cat eyes had lit up and she'd practically been licking her chops since Sam walked in the door. Not that Ally could blame her. Tuxedos were the dress code for the men on the lower level, and black was definitely Sam's color.

Ally was glad she'd worn the lace dress over Sam's objections. She remembered the club as being a hotbed of beautiful women. Ally was a realist about these things. She was a sex kitten only in her own imagination. The club's female staff was the real thing, and Ally needed a peekaboo lace dress just to hold her own.

"Put your mask on," Sam whispered.

Ally had almost forgotten. Angelic had been the manager even back in the days when Ally was here, and Ally couldn't run the risk of being recognized. Besides, all the women guests would be wearing masks. It was one of the club's many strange rules.

Ally had hooked the elaborately sequined black mask to the chain of her purse. She quickly slipped it on. Sam cupped Ally's elbow, and as they walked through a wall of laser lights, she realized that the anteroom itself was a metal detector. The security measures were much more rigorous than she remembered.

"This way," Sam said as the doors opened.

He pressed her elbow, urging her to come with him, but Ally needed a moment. She was startled by the club's dazzling new interior—and she'd just been hit by the reality of what they were about to do. She'd been fueled by nerves and adrenaline since she'd arrived in the city, and her reserves had just run out.

Suddenly the room was hot and bright. Everything went pale. Ally blinked, suddenly feeling unsteady. *Memories. There were too many of them here.*

Sam leaned close. "Are you all right?"

"Yes." She *had* to be. She couldn't let nerves get in her

way tonight. This was her only window of opportunity into the club. Jason was gone, and Sam had agreed to take her this one time.

"I thought I was getting a tour," she said, trying to sound eager. "Why are we standing here?"

If Sam hadn't taken her arm, she might have wavered. She didn't want him to know how paralyzed she'd been for those seconds—or to question his decision to help her. It had been a momentary lapse, and it wouldn't happen again.

The two of them drew curious looks as they made their way through the dazzling opulence of the foyer. Even with all the stunning women around, many of the men watched Ally with covetous eyes—as if she were a lemon drop, and their mouths were watering for something tart and sweet. It was enough to make her admit that Sam had been right. She shouldn't have worn such a revealing dress. Being the focus of any kind of attention was the last thing she needed tonight.

They passed the bar, and Sam asked if she wanted a drink, but Ally didn't trust herself not to spill it.

"He's transformed the place," she said, still trying to take in the changes. Jason had turned a lovely old cotton plantation into a palace. She couldn't imagine how much money he must have spent. But Jason wasn't one to stint on a dream—as long as it was his dream.

Sam had made late dinner reservations so they could go downstairs first. He'd revealed his plan to her as a two-parter. First, Ally would give him a clandestine tour of the lower level, including the passageway that would allow them to avoid the security entrance to the maze. Once they were in the maze, Ally would show him the location of the Vault and of Jason's sumptuous suite with its passageway to the safe room. Later that night, Sam would return and carry out some sort of grand diversion, the details which he was keeping to himself. While the entire club was in an uproar, he would breach the computer security system, get the evidence he needed, and then snatch Vix from her cell, taking her with him on his way out.

He wouldn't reveal his escape route, but Ally had heard of a tunnel that led from the lower level to the graveyard. Original to the house, it was very much a part of the ghost story lore. Jake Colby was believed to have sealed up the tunnel to prevent Micha from getting back into The Willows.

Sam's plan was complicated and risky. Ally's was very simple. She intended to make sure they'd located Vix *before* they left the club tonight. If necessary, she would trade clothes with her sister and let her leave with Sam. Then Sam could come back and rescue Ally.

As she walked with Sam toward the ornate wrought-iron cage that would take them to the lower level, Ally recognized the elevator operator. Monique had worked at the club when Ally was there, and unlike the other women, she'd had a brusque, no-nonsense manner. Ally didn't know much more about her than that, but if she'd recognized Monique, then Monique might just as easily recognize her.

Ally touched the bridge of her nose, making sure the mask was secure. It covered a great deal of her face, and she'd worn her hair piled on top of her head, which she'd never done when she was with Jason. But she hadn't expected her first test of fire to come so soon.

Monique greeted them with a polite nod, but gave no

sign of recognition. Still Ally was careful not to speak, aware that the sound of her voice might trigger a chord. Monique closed the creaky elevator doors the old-fashioned way, pulling them shut and latching them once Sam and Ally were in the cage.

A brushed steel door whistled down, sealing them in. Before they descended, she asked Ally to place her hand, palm-down, on the green screen in the console.

"She's a guest, not a member," Sam pointed out.

"Everyone has to be scanned," Monique said brusquely.

Ally caught Sam's nod telling her to go ahead. It was possible they'd do nothing more than check her fingerprints against a criminal database, in which case, they'd find nothing.

When Ally was done, Monique turned to Sam, every bit as officious. "Key, please."

Sam handed her his platinum key, and she inserted it into a slot on the elevator's control panel. As she turned the key, two red lights went off in quick sequence, followed by a green light. Monique pressed a pearlescent black bar, and the elevator started down.

Ally felt relief—and trepidation. Sam braced her with an arm around her waist. As the cage continued its slow descent to the lower level, she had a premonition that this might be a trap. She tried to push the thought out of her mind. Aragon was out of town, and according to Sam, he wasn't due back until tomorrow. So this evening was the perfect opportunity to find Vix.

Yet her sense of doom persisted. Ally felt as if she were descending into hell, and the devil himself was waiting for her down there. What if Aragon had actually planned it this way to get her back into the club?

She told herself to stop. There *were* real things to be frightened about. She could be recognized by someone on the staff or one of the older members. She and Sam might *not* even find Vix. But the image of Aragon lingered in her mind, and she knew it was because of what she'd seen on the lower level.

Decadence didn't begin to describe it. Jason went out of his way to grant his key club members their every wish and whim. The women who worked on the lower level were much more than hostesses. They were whatever their gentleman of the evening wanted them to be, including the spoils of the gaming tables.

Ally had been both sheltered as a child and sophisticated beyond her years. But she'd still been naive enough to be shocked by what she'd seen down there, and she didn't want her sister exposed to it. One night she'd been allowed to witness a card game with stakes that had appalled her. That had been the beginning of her deep disillusionment with Jason Aragon. He operated from the philosophy that people could be controlled by their weaknesses—and she feared he'd been proven right far too often.

No wonder Ally was envisioning doom. All of this had happened several years ago before Jason's vision had been fulfilled. She could hardly wrap her mind around what the lower level might have in store for them tonight.

THE BRUSHED STEEL DOOR slid up, and Monique opened the wrought-iron gate, ushering them out of the cage. Ally felt Sam's hand at her back as she stepped into a world she'd never seen before. The entire lower level was veiled by a transparent screen that seemed to be made of diamonds so tiny they formed a silvery mesh. Beyond the veil was a vast entertainment mecca shrouded in sparkling shadows.

Ally counted three massive arched portals. Her eye was drawn first to the one on the left. Beyond it was a bar and lounge that could have been a movie set. *Casablanca,* of course. The place was strangely enchanting. For a second she forgot to be apprehensive. She could see no sign of Aragon through the screen. That didn't mean he wasn't there, of course.

As she and Sam entered the lobby, Sam whispered, "Strut your stuff, lollipop."

Cue the nerves, she thought. She managed a wan smile, wondering how he stayed so calm when she felt like a bundle of nerves. But he didn't have the same baggage that she carried into this place. The club might be haunted, but it was her own ghosts she was facing tonight. Sam didn't have to worry about being recognized as Aragon's runaway girlfriend; nor did he have to put on a show as a sex kitten. That was Ally's role tonight, and it was up to her to buy the two of them enough time to search for Vix.

Sam seemed to sense her distress. He took her hand and his warm touch calmed her almost immediately. Thank God she wasn't alone.

Ally had no idea how much Jason had spent recreating the ambience of a Moroccan palace, but she'd heard rumors that it had cost millions of dollars, and that was back when millions actually meant something.

Jason had been born in Louisiana but Ally knew he'd spent most of his teenage years living with his uncle in Istanbul. It was a well-known secret at the club that at thirteen Jason had stabbed and killed a man who'd beaten his mother. To avoid prosecution, Jason had been whisked away to live with his uncle, a wealthy smuggler who had taken the boy as his own son and taught him everything he needed to know about running a criminal empire. After his uncle had died, Jason had moved what was now "his" empire to the United States. And he had brought some of that old-world Moorish decor with him.

Ally could see his early influences everywhere. The lobby beyond the curtain was open and spacious. Forming a crescent shape, the walls had been layered with a gold-tinted stucco. A hand-woven Turkish carpet covered the floor, and an elegantly carved dark mahogany cashier's station occupied the center of the room. Behind the cashier's station lay the lower level's main areas: the lounge, the gaming rooms and the spa.

Sam tugged on her hand and they headed toward the cashier's station. Two attractive women, both dressed in thirties-style, cut-on-the-bias gowns were there to greet them. Sam and the women exchanged pleasantries as he drew out a money clip and handed them a thick sheaf of bills. When the transaction was over he had two stacks of chips worth around ten thousand dollars.

Chips in hand, he turned to her. "Ready for a drink now?" he asked. "Champagne perhaps?"

"Definitely."

He appeared to be as impressed as she was with the lavish decor. "Keep in mind," he added, leaning close, "that I've never been in a casino that didn't have surveillance cameras everywhere. You can assume we're being watched every second."

"Right," Ally said.

Once inside the lounge, they walked to the bar where

Sam ordered a Bombay Sapphire on the rocks for himself and a glass of champagne for Ally. As she took a sip, she noticed Sam looking down at her over the rim of his cut-glass tumbler. His rugged features were softened by the whiskey-colored light, and the notion flickered through her thoughts that playing the adoring sex kitten might not be such a burden.

There were only a dozen or so couples in the lounge and another four on the dance floor. Of the women present, only half wore masks like Ally's. The others wore cloche hats with sheer silky veils indicating they were hostesses, not guests. A five-piece band, all but hidden in the darkest recesses of the lounge, was playing low, seductive music.

Ally noticed that they were still getting curious stares, possibly because they were the new couple. Sam leaned toward her. "I think we're being sized up. Turn on the heat."

It was time for Ally to play her part.

She set her drink on the bar and moved closer to Sam. Without a word passing between them, she laid her finger-tips on his chest and began provocatively toying with his silk tie. For anyone watching, the message to the other women would have been crystal clear. This is my man… hands off.

Sam managed to look almost bored. He did well at playing the part of the powerful man, so accustomed to adoration that it was almost an afterthought. Possibly he needed a wake-up call.

She moved in closer, snuggling her lips into the soft warm crease where his jaw met his neck. She caught the faint scent of cinnamon on his breath. From the deepest part of her throat, a sound filtered. It surprised her with its catlike vibration. Was she purring?

She hadn't known that she *could* purr.

Sam placed his hand on her hip and the heat of it seeped through her dress. She felt a fluttering sensation in the cleft between her legs. She'd stopped kidding herself that this was strictly about business. It still mystified her why she was reacting this way.

Was she having any effect on him? Or was she the only crazy one here?

Ally slid her hand down Sam's chest and along his hipbone. She didn't fail to notice that he was watching her from the corner of his eye. She smiled, letting her hand slide gently across his crotch. Not quite hard, but it would be soon with one more stroke, if that.

Sam leaned into her. His lips brushed her earlobe, sending a quiver down her spine. "You shouldn't touch things that you don't intend to play with later."

*Play with later...*

How wicked was that?

"I had to," she whispered.

"Had to?"

Ally glanced to her left. "There's a man over there who's staring at us. I had to let him know I wasn't available in case he had any thoughts about challenging you."

Sam's gaze drifted to the man loitering in the corner by himself. He was still staring. Ally didn't like the unmistakable smirk on his mouth.

"What do you mean challenging me?" Sam asked.

"It's a game Jason devised, and I can't imagine that he's not doing it still. It's too awful to explain. I'll have to show you." When she turned away from him, Sam snagged her arm and pulled her in close.

"Show me in a second. First, this—"

Sam buried his hand in her hair and pulled her head back, exposing her neck and mouth. His lips came down on hers and she nearly cried out from the sudden surge of pleasure rippling through her. His kiss was relentless, hungry and possessive, yet needy and, somehow, thrilling.

He had to stop kissing her this way. He was playing his role much too well. She was beginning to *feel* like an adoring sex kitten.

His gaze was piercingly sharp as he released her. "Think he got the message?"

Ally ran her tongue along her lips. They were literally tingling. "*Everybody* got the message."

"Good." Sam downed his drink. "Now, show me this awful game."

# *10*

ALLY WAS RELIEVED to see that the layout of the gaming area had changed very little as she led Sam through the arch linking the lounge and the casino. The high-stakes games were played on an elevated stagelike pedestal cordoned off by velvet ropes. That was where she and Sam were headed.

The casino itself was lined with mirrors in gilded frames and museum-quality art. There were no slot machines, but everything else was available from craps to roulette to the very traditional twenty-one. Jason had upgraded everything dramatically, Ally noted. The walls, floors and ceiling were fashioned from slabs of Italian marble with intricately carved friezes.

Within the confines of the high-stakes area, three chandeliers, sparkling like crystal bees' nests, hung over large mahogany tables. Dark green felt covered each table. Some had no players, yet a dealer stood at each, ready should a game develop. The busiest table had a half-dozen onlookers and two players stoically facing the other down.

"No-limit Hold 'Em," Sam said. "What's the big deal?"

They were a good twenty feet from the onlookers, but Ally lowered her voice. "The stakes, Sam. Watch."

Ally had never played the game, but she'd observed. At any point a player could announce "all in," meaning he was betting everything. If he lost, he and his money were gone. If he won, he usually won big. It was a game of skill and guts, no matter where it was played, but the club's game was unique.

"Any woman in the casino, hostess or guest, is fair game for a challenge match," she told Sam. "A member who's interested in someone else's female companion can issue a challenge for her. If the challenge is accepted, and they always are as a matter of honor, the female companion becomes the stakes. She's the prize. Of course, she has no say in the decision."

Sam shot her a glance. "No way."

"Yes," she assured him. "That woman in the sheer silver gown, standing next to the player with the dark glasses? She's up for grabs. If her gentleman friend loses this hand, she goes with the winner."

"To do what?"

"You can't be serious," she whispered. "Anything he damn well pleases, of course. He can't take her out of the club, but anything else goes."

"That's…sick."

"That's Jason Aragon," Ally replied.

As the dealer turned the last of the community cards over, Ally decided she'd seen enough. "I'm going to the ladies' room. I'll be back in a few minutes."

Sam reached for her arm, but caught a handful of the lace dress. "You can't go alone," he said.

"Don't be silly. Stay and watch your fellow man at his best. I'll be fine."

"Five minutes, and then I'm coming after you."

Ally flipped him the finger. She did it so quickly no one could have seen it, probably not even him, but it was the thought that counted. He was getting too good at this king-of-the-world thing.

"The longer I'm gone," she reminded him, "the less likely it is that someone will challenge you."

She left him with that thought and walked out to the lobby. She glanced in either direction, then went down the hallway to the ladies' room. The maze was on the other side of the hallway, behind the elevator bank, the entrance secured by guards. Ally had found an old passageway leading into a room in the maze when she'd been searching for a way out. *Please let that passageway still exist,* she thought. *And let me remember where it was.*

An odd sound was coming from an adjoining hallway up ahead of Ally. It sounded like someone was weeping. Curious, she passed the ladies' room and continued on. A gust of freezing air brought her to a halt in the intersection of the two hallways. Down the adjoining one to her left was a woman in a long white gown.

Ally felt as if all the blood were draining from her body. She was too far away to see the woman clearly, but a sense of terror gripped her. She forced herself to move anyway. Something compelled her to go after the woman, even as she watched her open a door on the hallway and vanish.

Ally was breathing hard by the time she got to the door. She opened it to utter darkness and the lingering scent of roses. She couldn't see anything, but something told her this was it, the room with the passageway. Again, she heard the sound of a woman weeping. But this time it was her, weeping with relief.

SAM OBSERVED the challenge game with a mixture of fascination and disgust. He had played cash games for sky-high stakes, but nothing like this. He knew, as did the player wearing the shades, that the game was already lost. His female companion, whoever she was, would go to the challenger. Interesting that she didn't seem to be bothered by the prospect, but that could be an act.

Sam wondered if there would be a fight or at least an argument over her. Good sportsmanship in a situation like this was hard to imagine. As the final card fell, the loser rose and escorted her to the winner, handing her over like a racehorse at auction. When the men shook hands, Sam actually thought he might be ill.

Another good reason to shut down this operation.

"Ah, Mr. Sinclair, so you finally came down to spend some time with us." Sam turned to see Angelic gliding toward him, stunning as always in a halter-neck turquoise gown that fit her to perfection. Interesting accessories, too. Her cell phone mouthpiece was studded with tiny turquoise gemstones.

Angelic clearly enjoyed drawing attention to herself— and she was nobody's fool. Looks were as important as brains in a place like this, and she knew it. She was as accomplished in the bedroom as the boardroom, and she dressed to get that across.

She offered her hand, which he brought to his lips. "The most beautiful woman in the room," he said.

Her eyebrow arched with pleasure that seemed genuine, and at the same time, her tone was professional and discreet. "I have a message from Mr. Aragon," she said. "He'd like to meet with you regarding the problem you discussed. He has information that might be of interest."

"And has he told you what that problem is?"

"No, of course not! I just pass on messages—and make sure *everything* runs smoothly."

Sam caught the emphasis. He looked over at the gaming table that was empty now that the prize had been won—and collected. "Quite a game. I hear it was Jason's brainchild."

"In fact, it was mine." Angelic moved in closer and Sam caught the light fragrance of her perfume. "Want to know a secret, Sam?"

"Always," he replied, noting that she'd switched to his first name.

She lowered her voice. "It's not true of all the women who end up being prizes in a challenge match, but it is true for many that they find the whole experience quite exciting."

"Really?"

Her dark eyes flashed with affirmation. "It's being the object of that much desire, I believe. Having two men do battle over you is stimulating in a very primal and primitive way. I think it unleashes an eroticism in many women they didn't know existed."

Sam merely nodded. Apparently she'd given the subject some thought or had been a prize herself at one time and spoke from firsthand experience. Sam still considered it demeaning. No one should be dehumanized to the point of being a sex prize. However, he kept his opinion to himself. He had a cover to protect.

"Speaking of beautiful women," Angelic said. "Where's the friend you mentioned? Didn't she come with you?"

He was beginning to wonder about his friend, too. "She went to the ladies' room."

"Really? I just came from there. Odd that I didn't see her. There wasn't anyone but me there."

Sam didn't like the sound of that—or the questions in Angelic's expression. He checked his watch and saw that Ally had been gone well over the five-minute limit he'd given her. He didn't want her wandering around on her own. For someone educated in the best private schools, she seemed to be missing some of the more basic genes, like the one for impulse control. He didn't want to think about the consequences of losing control—he'd been living with them since yesterday.

Angelic's cell rang, and at the same time, the entire casino began to pulse with red light. A siren ripped through the silence, and everyone in the room froze, including Sam.

He had a feeling Ally had already lost control…of something.

Angelic was still talking on the phone in furiously low tones, and Sam glanced over her shoulder to see Ally peeking into the room from behind the arched doorway to the bar. He shook his head, telling her to stay where she was. She nodded and backed out of sight just as a contingent of security guards poured into the casino.

"There's been some kind of breach," Angelic said into the cell mouthpiece. "Post security at the exits and check IDs. Detain anyone in question. I'll handle this level."

She nodded reassuringly to Sam, but her smile was too quick, too bright. "Excuse me," she told him. "I need a minute with my team. Sorry for the inconvenience. Please go on over to the bar and have some champagne."

She extended the same offer to the remaining gamblers. "Cristal on the house!" she called out, still smiling brightly. "We appreciate your patience, and we'll have this cleared up in no time."

Angelic continued to talk on the phone as she gathered

her security team together in a corner of the casino. Sam went to the lounge to find Ally and learn what had happened. The security breach didn't appear to have anything to do with the gambling operation itself. He almost wished it had.

Ally was at the bar, drinking champagne. "Where were you?" he whispered as he sat on the seat next to her. "And don't tell me the bathroom. I made the mistake of telling Angelic that was where you were, and she'd just come from there."

"Stop yelling at me," Ally said. She took a drink of champagne, and he could see that her hands were shaking.

"I'm not yelling at you. I'm whispering."

"Maybe, but you want to yell."

Sam sighed—and started again. "Did you just trigger the security system?"

"It may have been me," she said evasively.

"It *was* you. What did you do?"

Her tone was prickly. "The layout down here is different now. I needed to have a look around."

"And did you find the passageway into the maze? What about the Vault? Did you find it?"

She studied the bubbles in the champagne. "I may have."

"Where is it? I'll come back tomorrow. We can't do anything else tonight. The place is crawling with security."

"I'm not telling you where the Vault is until my sister's out of this flesh factory. I don't have any other way to protect her."

Sam's gut tightened. She wasn't really going to try and outplay him, was she? "You don't believe that I'll find your sister and get her out of here?"

She glared at him. "How do I know you won't get the evidence you need and vanish? What's to stop you? And if Jason had *your* sister would you trust me? Of course you wouldn't. You'd use whatever leverage you had, which is all I'm doing. So don't yell at me."

Sam felt the blood rushing to his face. He couldn't remember the last time that had happened. There were times he'd wondered if he had any blood left, but she certainly had ways of reminding him.

"You have to trust me," he said, his voice low and emphatic. "I need to know where that passageway is. Otherwise, how am I supposed to get into the maze to find your sister?"

"I'm certain Vix is being held in the safe room where Jason held me. I can tell you where it is. But I won't tell you where the Vault is until you get my sister out of here. That's the only way I'm doing this."

"In that case, deal's off. We agreed that we would locate the rooms, and that I would come back and carry out both missions."

"That was *your* plan. I didn't get a vote, nor did I agree to anything. And this is *not* the place to discuss this."

He sighed and took a look around. She was right. What he had to do was get them both out of here without any more incidents, which meant escorting his girlfriend out the front door, exactly as he would have if the breach hadn't happened. He would say the alarms had frightened Ally, and jokingly suggest the club hire a ghostbuster to keep their apparitions under control.

Sam's real challenge was much thornier than making an exit. He needed the information Ally had, and it didn't look like he was going to get it by any normal means. His thoughts took a darker turn as options screened through his mind. Only one of them made sense. Torture, he mused with some satisfaction. It was fast and effective. And it *had* to be easier than trying to gain her trust.

ALLY SKIMMED the message again, hardly able to believe what she was reading.

> Sorry about that crazy e-mail I sent you. I'm
> not really being held against my will. Dumb
> joke, huh? Everything's okay, I just need a little
> time to myself. Don't worry about me. I'll be
> in touch soon. Victoria.

Her sister had sent another e-mail, but Ally didn't know what to make of it. Now Vix was saying she was fine? It was all a mistake?

Ally stared at her laptop screen. The message sounded like Vix, but why was there no mention of Jason? Could he have put her up to it? Ally found it hard to believe that her sister would pull a stunt like this. Then again, it wouldn't be the first time. Vix had a bad habit of ditching when she wasn't getting her way, and she'd started very young. They'd actually lived in a palace with guards before the family was driven into exile, and Vix had managed to sneak out of the place several times.

Ally saved the message, turned off her computer and sat at the desk, trying to figure out what to do next. She and Sam had come straight back to the suite after the security fiasco, but Sam had gone into his reflective mode, completely shutting her out. She'd left him in the living room, staring at the pattern in the carpet, and she'd gone to the bedroom to check her e-mail. That was nearly an hour ago. It was now 1:00 a.m., and he was either furious, or furiously working on another plan that would leave her and her sister out in the cold.

She couldn't tell him about the message. She wasn't sure she believed, but he might. He might even use it as an excuse to abandon the mission, if he hadn't already decided to do so. Her stomach was one big knot as she contemplated giving up now. That couldn't happen. They had to go through with their plans as if this e-mail didn't exist.

Ally got up from the desk, aware that she was trembling. It was adrenaline, but it was determination, too. She was going to take a hot bath, and pray for strength.

Moments later, she sat on the edge of the whirlpool tub and turned on the water, wondering why she'd bothered to put on the sheer red kimono and gown. She'd told herself it was just a precaution in case the suite was still rigged with cameras. She certainly had no other reason to wear lingerie.

She wiggled her fingers in the cascading water, deciding it wasn't hot enough. She wanted to soak herself into oblivion tonight. Her temples throbbed, and she'd come up with nothing to resolve the impasse with Sam.

Suddenly a hand snaked around her and turned the water pressure down. Sam had come in from the bedroom, and his forearm brushed hers as he adjusted the faucet to the flow he wanted.

"I like it hot," she said, startled at how close he was as he leaned over her. Now *why* had she said that? He sank down, sitting next to her, and she could feel the heat from his bare chest through the sheer material of her kimono. As far as she could tell, he wore only his pajama bottoms.

"We can talk," he said, sitting right behind her, "as long as we keep it low. The water should muffle our words."

"Talk about what?"

"About what happened at the club tonight."

He probably wanted her to apologize, and she might if she'd thought if would make any difference. He'd refused to understand that this wasn't about not trusting him. It was about Vix's welfare, and Ally needed some insurance. It surprised her how much she did trust Sam. Still she couldn't take risks with her sister's well being.

"Can you hear me?" he said.

Ally nodded. The opposite wall of the tub was mirrored and she could see both of them. His lips were less than an inch from her ear as he spoke. The soft rush of air on her earlobe tickled.

"Is the place still bugged?" she asked him.

"The camera in the bedroom is gone. I haven't come across anything else, but that doesn't mean they're not using equipment too sophisticated for my detector."

"So, what do we do?"

"What we've been doing all along. I found a bug in the Porsche on the way home from the club tonight, which means they haven't given up."

She glanced around at him. "And you didn't tell me?"

"There was no need. We weren't speaking."

She smiled. In the quiet that followed, she realized they were probably going to be bedmates again. The thought made her acutely aware of everything about him, including a tantalizing hint of cinnamon fragrance. Had to be toothpaste. Nobody chewed gum at this time of night.

She got up, thinking he would back off and give her some space, but when she turned to face him, she found herself in full frontal contact with his body. With the edge of the tub enclosure pressed against her butt and Sam pressed against her breasts, there was no room to spare. Hardly room to breathe.

"Listen carefully," he told her, still whispering. "This is important. I'll get your sister out of the club, but once that's done, I want the location of the Vault, and if I find that you've compromised me or my mission in any way, I'll personally escort both you and your sister back to the flesh factory and hand you over to Aragon. Understood?"

"Sam, thank you!" She could hardly believe he'd given into her demands. There had to be a catch, but she wasn't going to let herself think about that right now—or his threat. She wanted her sister out of there first, and then maybe she'd tell him about the e-mail. He wouldn't really throw her and Vix to the wolves. He was bluffing. What else could he do?

"Don't be so free with your gratitude," he muttered. "I'm deadly serious. I'll hand you over to Aragon myself."

"Of course, you will!"

His brooding stare warned her not to shower him with tears and kisses, as if she wanted to. Instead she squeezed his arm, wondering if he could possibly imagine how grateful she actually was.

"I need sleep," he said. "I'll take the couch in the living room. You can have the bed."

"The bed?"

He glowered at her. "You want the couch?"

*"Sam."* She yanked him close, her breath whistling in her throat. "We can't sleep separately. If there's even a

possibility that we're being bugged, we have to stick with the lovers thing. You just said that yourself."

"I'm willing to chance it." He stifled a yawn. "I checked the place out pretty thoroughly. I think we're okay."

"Chance it? No way. I refuse to be half-assed when my sister's life is at stake. We're going to do this right."

He wasn't taking her seriously. He was just going through the motions, just trying to appease her. Maybe he was discouraged by tonight's fiasco, and he no longer believed they could pull it off. She had to make him see that they could. They were a team. They were going to win. Game on.

A plan came to mind, and the more Ally thought about it, the less drastic it seemed.

She hesitated, not sure how to say it. "Sam, we can't blow it now. Not when we're so close. If anything, we need to raise our game. I'm deadly serious about this. I think we should—you know—do it."

"Do what?"

Evidently, he *didn't* know. "Have sex, of course."

He just looked at her. Not a word. Just looked.

"Now, listen to me," she said, "because *this* is important. Your credibility is at stake here. No Casablanca man brings a female companion to bed so he can roll over and fall asleep."

"Christ, woman, can't you ever give it a rest?" He gave a weary shake of his head. "I'm on a case. I can't have sex with you. I never mix business with pleasure, and even if I did, I wouldn't...not with you."

"What's wrong with me?" Ally stepped back, squinting at him. "I said what's wrong with me?"

He yanked her back and held her close, hissing in her ear. "Lovers, not fighters, okay?"

"I don't mix business with pleasure, either," she whispered back, "but I don't consider this pleasure. It's business for me, too. And it could be life or death for Vix. We don't have to have real sex. All we have to do is pretend. You can do that, can't you?"

"Pretend? Like get under the covers and make noises?"

"Well, a little more realism than that. The way they do it in the movies."

"In the movies they get naked and hump each other."

"Well, yes, but it's not real. It just looks real—for the cameras."

"There are no cameras here!"

"There might be. You don't know that for sure—and I told you, I'm not taking that chance. Now, stop being silly. Be a man."

Sam was looking at her in a completely different way now, as if he were the one coming up with a drastic plan—and it probably had something to do with his hands around her skinny neck. In apparent frustration, he fished in his pajama pocket and pulled out a stick of Dentyne. There was the source of the spicy cinnamon smell.

"Hell, why not," he said. "Let's pretend. But just remember when I get a hard-on? My penis is only pretending."

"And you remember the same thing when I'm draping myself all over you and showering you with kisses and sweet nothings. This isn't personal. I'm not interested in getting close to a man like you."

Sam popped the gum in his mouth. His eyebrows knit. "A man like me? What's that supposed to mean?"

There were at least a dozen different answers to that question, and most of them would get her into trouble if she voiced them: Sexy, exciting, dangerous to the heart, the mind and the orderly life she'd been living up until now.

She opted for the one that she hoped would put the brakes on his testosterone levels. "Some men fall into the category of undesirables."

Sam laughed. "I've never been called that before."

"If a man has trouble written all over him, what else would you call him?"

"Me? Trouble?"

"You. Trouble. And intimacy-phobic."

Her gaze was riveted to his jaw and his mouth and the way he was working over that damn piece of gum. Of all the sexual enticements in the world, why did hers have to be the smell of Red Hots on a man's breath?

And now, the one man on earth that she should *not* be attracted to carried that same scent on him daily...and nightly. It just wasn't fair.

Sam wadded the gum wrapper and flicked it into the wastebasket. "All right," he said, "bedtime. I'll go turn out the lights and lock the doors."

He turned and left her standing there. Breathless.

What had she gotten herself into now? Sam Sinclair and Red-Hots breath and bedtime! What a combo.

# *11*

As Sam went about the business of locking the suite and turning off the lights, Ally took off her robe, drew back the comforter and slipped into bed. When Sam walked into the room, she smiled at him and patted the pillow next to her.

"Come to bed," she cooed, curling up like a kitten, "I need a little whammy, Sammy."

Rolling his eyes, Sam climbed into bed. He stretched out on his back, and threw a hand over his head, revealing bulging biceps and the feathery golden hair of his underarm.

Ally cuddled next to him and rested her hand on his chest, working her fingers into his silky chest hair. "Everything I'm about to do is fake," she whispered. "So don't get any ideas that I'm coming on to you."

"The thought never entered my mind." He shut off the bedside lamp, but the full moon outside the window shimmered like a Japanese lantern. "All right," he whispered, rolling back to her, "let's get this over with. Big day tomorrow. I need my sleep."

Ally was torn for a moment. The last thing she wanted was to throw him off his stride tomorrow, but something inside her prickled at his indifference.

She sat up and made a show of slipping off her gown and tossing it to the floor. The room was dark enough that she couldn't see Sam's features distinctly, though the moonlight silhouetted his powerful body.

She eased down next to him, her nipples coming into contact with his bare chest. When she moved the sensation of raking her buds across his chest was intoxicating. She felt warmth on the small of her back and realized it was his palm. He'd put his arm around her. Leaning into him she began nibbling the curve of his neck. Between his palm, his chest and his neck, she felt enveloped by his intense body heat.

Lord that felt good.

Whether by design or accident, she didn't know, but she felt Sam's grasp around her waist tighten and draw her closer to him. She took his earlobe into her mouth and began sucking on it, teasing it with little flicks of her tongue. He moaned softly.

Was that the moan of a tired man? She thought not.

Whether it was a wild-child impulse from her past or her strong sexual response to him, she was on the brink of doing something slightly outrageous—and to her surprise, she gave into it with no hesitation.

Her hand was resting on his chest, her fingers tracing small circles. Moving in close, she draped her bare leg over his. "Oh, Sam, you still have your pajama bottoms on," she said loud enough to be overheard.

She eased her hand down his chest and onto the fly of his pajamas. His erection was hard and unyielding, and she could feel it throbbing beneath her palm. She leaned close to his ear. "Well, that didn't take long," she whispered teasingly. "Still sleepy?"

"Oh, you bitch," he replied, his voice equally soft.

"You betcha." She smiled.

She wrapped her fingers around his engorged penis and squeezed. Sam's body tightened, and his voice became a low growl.

"Let me get you out of these," she offered sweetly.

Before he could reply, she was on her knees and tugging his pajama bottoms down his legs. She threw them to the floor and slipped back under the covers with him. "Now, isn't that better?"

Sam uttered a primal noise that she took as a yes.

"Let me take care of you, baby," she said.

They were both naked now, hidden only by the sheets and the comforter. She pressed her body against his, reveling in the scent of male arousal and cinnamon candy, an irresistible mix. This felt natural, even though that seemed impossible, given everything that was going on. Then again, maybe that was the reason. In the midst of all this uncertainty and fear, it was only when she was with him that she could distract herself from her concern about Vix.

Murmuring his name, she snuggled closer, but he didn't respond. Her frustration was sharpened by disappointment. He didn't want to cooperate. Evidently she was going to carry out this charade for both of them.

She got up and straddled his torso, pulling the comforter up around her shoulders. She had not worn panties to bed. It had seemed silly to put them on under such a sheer, sexy gown. But that may have been a mistake she realized as she sat down.

First her bare bottom and then her bare lips came into contact with Sam's warm, hard body. Every little move she made sent bolts of electricity through her clitoris and into the pit of her belly as she felt his shaft press against her.

Sam lightly caressed her thighs, and Ally's sharp breath made her dizzy. Her thighs tightened and ached. The sensation climbed upward, radiating pleasure. Hot, steamy pleasure. She felt a warm gush of excitement between her legs, and that excited her more.

She leaned down and kissed him hard and long, and he didn't seem to object. His arms enclosed her, pulling her closer and closer until her breasts pillowed against his chest. Her nipples yearned to be kissed as hard as her lips.

Ally broke the kiss and sat up, brushing flyaway hair from her face. It was the only way to maintain any control at all. Her mouth had gone dry. She could hear soft panting, but it was his.

Sam ran his hands along her sides and onto her breasts. He cupped them, doing nothing but that, holding her, and it was thrilling. His thumbs played against her swollen nipples, teasing them as she had teased his earlobe earlier. When she moved her hips, another bolt struck like lightning. It felt like a miniorgasm, and she had to literally capture a groan behind her clenched lips.

She couldn't take much more of this.

She began inching backward, still holding the comforter up to her shoulders. As she shifted, Sam's erection was forced back and down as she rode over it. As the tip of it slid along her moist, sensitive flesh she smothered a gasp. The way it throbbed against her was pure torture.

She hurried over the danger zone and stopped when she got to his knees. She pulled the comforter over her head, trying to compose herself, which wasn't easy.

She dropped to one hand and accidentally grazed his

penis with her cheek as she lowered her head. It was hard
to see, but she was clearly on the mark, so to speak. If
anyone were watching, they would have to assume that she
had taken him into her mouth.

It was becoming difficult to convince herself that this
was only a means to an end, especially with the way she
was responding to him. He seemed reasonably assured
that they weren't under surveillance. Why wasn't she?
They would both have been asleep by now, in separate
rooms. But it all came back to the same thing. He didn't
have a missing sister.

She had to make this look real.

She was in complete darkness under the comforter,
which made things a little easier, although she could sense
the outline of his body as if it had an electrical field. She
took his shaft into her hands and bent toward it. She could
feel the heat from his lower body rising up and flowing
over her. With his member in hand, she began to bob
slowly up and down, but with her head to the side of him.

Sam's erection pulsed. She could feel it growing,
stretching her curled fingers. Hoping to keep things under
control, she wrapped one hand around the very bottom of
his shaft, and then placed her other hand just above it. But
even with both hands, she couldn't quite contain him.

What would all that pulsating muscle feel like, she
wondered.

He must be in agony by now. The thought lit a tiny
spark of pleasure. Even so, enough was enough.

She came out from under the comforter, pretending to
lick her lips. It was wicked of her, but she couldn't resist.

Sam was breathing hard and his eyes were closed. He
seemed barely aware of her as she scooted up his legs, the

comforter still draped over her shoulders. Ally made a show of rising up once she was close enough to his shaft to make it believable. She lowered her body, pretending to be impaling herself on him, and sighed loudly, wildly.

"Oh, Sammy," she cried, "you feel wonderful."

Again, she used the comforter to hide herself as she simulated the movements of a woman riding her man. It wasn't easy to navigate with his erection in her way, but the sensations as it brushed her bottom were amazing. Sweet friction.

She had never ached so badly to have a man inside her.

"Ally," he whispered, "you have to stop."

"In a sec." She gave herself thirty seconds to compose herself. She wanted to stop but couldn't seem to make that happen. Her hips were moving involuntarily now. She began counting down when Sam did something completely unexpected. He placed his hands on her swollen breasts and squeezed her nipples. The sharpness of it brought Ally up, her thighs quivering. But she came down just as fast, and suddenly Sam's member was sliding easily—and accidentally—inside her.

For a nanosecond there existed the possibility of getting off him, but the thought barely registered. Ally ground her hips down hard and squeezed her inner muscles, the sensation exquisite. She bit down on her lip, but even that couldn't stop the deep, lingering moan that came from her throat.

He caught her by the waist, and she felt the power of his upper body as he brought her down and lifted her. She thought he was going to guide her in the wild mating dance that had overtaken her, however his jaw was clenched with something near agony. He pulled her off him and brought her down to lay beside him.

"What about the word *stop* don't you understand?" he ground out.

Ally couldn't find the breath to answer him. She'd been teased to the point of torment, too, and all she could do was moan. He was lucky she wasn't writhing. She was feeling sensations she didn't known existed. She needed to climax, her body throbbed for that completion. But she knew he was right. They had to stop.

Sam threw the comforter off and got out of bed. He headed for the master bath. "I need a shower," he muttered. He didn't have to tell her that this would be a cold one.

The sound of splashing water told Ally that he was in the shower. She hazarded a glance toward the bathroom door. Since he'd shut it so hard it had swung back open, she could see him through the glass shower doors.

His back was to her, but she had the impression that he might be doing something besides soaping himself down. Masturbating? Was he turned on to the point that even a cold shower couldn't cool him down? And had she done that to him?

Her own hand stole down between her legs. She found the swollen nub and felt a searing flash of pleasure. Her stomach muscles clenched, causing her to curl up and moan.

She was under the comforter so if anyone were looking they wouldn't see anything as she began to touch herself. Her body was aching, simply aching. Almost like a thief planning to steal something in the dark, she stroked the tender area, urging her body toward its own climax. Even as the tension built, she knew this wasn't what she really needed. She needed his mouth on hers, his body in hers.

A small orgasm shot through her suddenly, but that only seemed to make it worse. Ally applied more pressure, determined to end the misery, but just as she felt herself getting close, Sam shut off the water and the shower door banged open. She quickly pulled her hand away, not wanting to be caught.

Frustrated, she rolled to her side and jerked the comforter up to her chin. If there were surveillance bugs in this place, Sam had to find them tomorrow. There was no way on earth she going through this again.

SHE WASN'T IN BED when Sam woke up the next morning. For some reason that panicked him. Probably for lots of reasons, he realized. His chest felt weirdly hollow as he threw off the covers. His pajama bottoms had come loose and were falling off him as he strode across the bedroom carpet. He yanked them up and knotted the tie.

No one answered when he rapped on the master bathroom door, so he nudged it open. She wasn't there. She wasn't in the guest bathroom or the sitting room, either.

Sam turned around in the middle of the sitting room, scanning every nook and cranny for clues. Had she left? Voluntarily?

Coffee. The pungent aroma wafted from the wet bar, where he sighted a freshly made pot. She had to be here somewhere. No one else would have made coffee. He went to investigate.

He found her out on the terrace off the sitting room. She was perched on a wrought-iron chair at the patio table, bent over her laptop computer and trying to read the screen in the late morning sunshine. Her cup of coffee sat teetering in its saucer. The table's umbrella provided partial shade but it was already hot and bright outside. Probably getting close to noon. He'd slept late.

He watched her from the doorway, somehow pleased at the sight of her in one of the hotel's big fluffy white robes. She was barefoot and bare-legged, probably bare everywhere underneath the robe. It wasn't difficult to imagine the plush terry cloth lightly caressing her skin. The mere thought turned him on like a son of a bitch. That silky skin of hers had been all over him last night.

"What are you doing?" he asked.

"Checking my e-mail," she said, glued to the screen.

"Anything from your sister?"

She glanced up abruptly. It had seemed like the most obvious question he could have asked, but she was alarmed by it. That made him curious.

"No, nothing." With a couple quick taps, she shut the computer off and closed the lid.

"You were sleeping hard," she said, picking up her coffee cup, "so I came out here."

Sleeping hard. Interesting choice of words. The last part was true, but he hadn't slept until some time toward dawn.

Now that he knew she was okay he could be pissed again. And he was, but probably at himself for getting frightened. He didn't like the options that had run through his mind. The thought of her leaving voluntarily had been almost as disturbing as the thought of someone taking her.

Massively inconvenient, he told himself. Everything about her was massively inconvenient. While he'd been looking for her, he'd also scanned the place again f or bugs. There weren't any. He was almost certain of it, which meant the entire hassle of last night was unnecessary. They hadn't had to get naked and have pretend sex that had turned into the real thing. All except for the climax.

"I made some coffee," she said. "Help yourself."

"I will."

The silence stretched until she finally realized that he was looking at her. In a gesture that surprised him with its offhand charm, she tilted her head slightly. "What?" she asked.

"Nothing. Just admiring the view."

She turned steamy pink. "Isn't it lovely," she said, gesturing toward the hotel grounds where the magnolia trees were loaded down with gorgeous creamy white flowers.

They both knew he wasn't referring to that view.

"Coffee's great. Help yourself," she said again.

"I *will.*"

She seemed to be trying to ignore him, so he decided to make that impossible for her. He walked over and sat on the arm of her chair. "The coffee couldn't be better than this," he said, tilting her chin up and kissing her lightly. Her lips tasted of French roast coffee and cream.

She drew back and clutched the terry lapel together.

He smiled and took her hand away, letting the robe fall open again. "Why ruin the view," he said.

He stared straight into her eyes as he stroked her throat and traced her collarbone, and then he slipped his hand inside the robe to cup her breast. It was achingly hot to the touch. He flicked her nipple with his thumbnail and watched her eyes change. They darkened like melting chocolate. She was beautiful, dammit. He didn't need coffee or sleep. He needed her.

"What in H are you doing?" she said, raspy-voiced.

"Helping myself." He shrugged. "You told me to. Thought you might want another whammy…this morning."

"Last night's was sufficient."

"Really? For me it wasn't sufficient at all. I'd like to fuck you right there in that chair."

Her mouth dropped open, and her eyes got as wide as her coffee saucer.

He mouthed the words, "Not a great expression for the cameras."

Recognition flooded her. "Cameras," she said under her breath. She sprang up and took his hand, gracing him with a sensual smile as she led him over to the terrace railing.

As they looked out at the magnolias, she moved closer to him. "Pretend we're making out," she said. "I have something to tell you, and it's important."

She snuggled into the crook of his shoulder and played with the string on his pajama bottoms. Sam said nothing, but his body responded eagerly to the way she worked her fingers inside his waistband and played in the hair that feathered his belly. She must have taken the advanced courses in sexual crazy-making. She was waking the lion, of course.

Damn traitorous penis. It liked her better than it liked him.

"What's so important," he whispered, "besides playing with my pants?"

She looked up at him seemingly perturbed at the accusation. "I think you should go over to the club now. It's not open, and you won't have to worry about the crowds. You'll have the run of the place."

"I'm not worried about the crowds, Ally. The crowds are my cover. Otherwise, I might as well have a bull's-eye on my back."

"We can't wait until tonight. We need to get Vix out of there. Jason's due back. We're running out of time."

"So you want me to break into the club this morning? That's probably not the best idea you've ever had."

"You said you were a government agent."

"That doesn't make me the invisible man. The security guards are there in full force whether the club's open or not. Perhaps you didn't notice Aragon's state-of-the-art security system?"

"Then what are you going to do?"

"I'll go over this evening, at seven or eight, as I always do. I'm not going to draw attention to myself with any sudden changes."

She wasn't happy with him, but that was fine. He wasn't happy with her, either. "There are some other things I need to take care of first, anyway," he said.

"What things?"

"Research that has to be done."

"Research on the club?"

"You could call it that."

"I can help you."

"You can't, but I'm taking you along anyway. I've known you, what…forty-eight hours? But it's long enough to know that you can't be left on your own."

"Oh, like I'm a child?"

"No, like you're a desperate sibling who wants to free her sister at all costs. You can't be trusted."

She sighed heavily. "Where are we going?"

He released her and kissed her on the forehead,

although he would have preferred his lips to be anywhere else. "You'll see when we get there. Dress for the weather. They're predicting thunder and lightning this afternoon."

ALLY'S PATIENCE was running thin. She'd been sitting in the lobby of the county library for going on forty minutes and she had no idea why they were there. He'd said next to nothing on the trip over here beyond what he'd already mentioned about doing some research. The only thing he'd been clear about was that she should wait in the lobby.

"Don't move until I get back," he'd said as he disappeared into the library.

Well, she'd been a good girl. She hadn't moved from the bench with the hard plastic cushion and now her butt was asleep. She needed to get up and stretch, find a water faucet and wet her parched throat. The weather was making her nervous, too. Through the lobby doors she'd watched the sky go from clear to ominously dark. Most of all, she wanted to know what Sam was up to.

She stopped at the information desk, and a bubbly young aide pointed her toward the reference section on the far side of the library.

Ally spotted Sam almost as soon as she entered the stacks. He hadn't seen her yet. He was walking toward a high table and leafing through a bound hardcover volume that looked as if it might be some kind of history book. He set the book on the table and flipped to the back pages.

Ally edged up behind him, trying to see what he was reading and wondering how close she could get before he noticed her. It did look like a history book of some kind, and she had a hunch he was going through the index, but she wanted to see for herself.

She got as close to see that she was right about the book.

"Why did you leave your post?" he asked without looking up.

She started to explain, but countered instead with, "What are you reading?" He couldn't very well create a scene and make her go back to the lobby. They were in a public library.

"I'm looking for whatever I can find on Club Casablanca, formerly known as The Willows."

"The Willows," she echoed. "I've always loved that name. Conjures up thoughts of magnolia trees and mint juleps."

"Conjures up thoughts of blackmail, deceit and betrayal," he muttered.

"Are you talking about Jason?"

He shook his head dismissively and went back to his task. "You didn't answer my question. Why did you leave your post?"

"To avoid peeing my pants?" It was a better excuse than a sleepy butt.

Finally he deigned to look at her. She almost wished he hadn't. He really could get overbearing with the orders.

"Hit the bathroom and get back to your post," he said.

She snapped to attention. "Yes, sir. Thank you, *sir*."

That he ignored, which was exactly what she hoped he'd do. It gave her the opportunity to disappear around the corner and into the next aisle where she could rearrange the books on the shelf to create an opening and do a little spying.

She made a space on a shelf at eye level and saw him jotting notes on the page he was reading. Defacing library property? She should report him. He shocked her still more when he ripped out that page and the adjacent one, and stuffed both inside his jacket. Now she knew why he'd worn a jacket on what must be the muggiest day of the year. She was expecting to hear a thunderclap at any moment.

Interesting that he could have had a photocopy of whatever he wanted from the book but he hadn't done it, which probably meant he didn't want his interest in the material known. She ducked as he turned toward her and put the book in the space she'd made. Obviously not where it belonged. Through the open crack that was left, she could see him heading for the lobby and realized she was in trouble. He was on his way to find her.

She had to work fast. She wanted to get her hands on the pages he'd hidden in his jacket. For now she would check out the book he'd been going through. She pulled it off the shelf from her side, noting that it looked clean and new. It was a recently published historical account of the region.

The section with the ripped-out pages was easy to find. Ally wasn't surprised to discover that he'd been reading about the Wolverton family and their dispute with the Colbys. He'd already said he was looking for information on The Willows. Somehow that haunted house seemed to play into his investigation. If it were important enough for him to rip pages out of a book and take them with him, she wanted to know why.

# *12*

SHE SPOTTED Sam in the lobby, his hands on his hips. He was obviously looking for her, and by his expression, he wasn't happy. But she could also see the tension etched into his features, and it made her wonder if he were worried about her or the mission.

"Over here," she said, waving as she hurried toward him.

His relief was so evident that it made her heart pound. Possibly—just possibly—he'd answered her question.

"Sorry that took so long," she said as she reached him.

"Come on." He gripped her hand possessively. "We have to go."

Something had him in a big hurry. She was glad he hadn't questioned her about being gone so long but she had no idea why they were running toward the door.

"Is there someone here you don't want to see?" she asked.

"There's a bad storm brewing. We need to beat it."

"Where are we going?"

"I'll explain later."

Ally was getting tired of his man-of-few-words thing, but as they dashed out the door, she saw the dark clouds, now roiling overhead. The area was known for its thunderstorms and this one looked like something out of a disaster movie. She waited at the entrance while he brought the Porsche around, and by the time they'd roared off, the sky had turned as yellow and black as an ugly bruise.

They'd only driven a few blocks when she realized they weren't heading back to the hotel. They were in an older, picturesque section of town where the roads were lined with two-story buildings resembling old-fashioned rooming houses. Other than the cars parked at the curb and a few rather garish neon signs in storefront windows, it looked like a postcard of mid-nineteenth-century New Orleans. Even the gaslight-styled streetlamps with their wide glass domes seemed to have come from that era.

But what caught her eye were the French Quarter-style balconies. Each rooming house had one, encircled by graceful wrought-iron rails. Louvered doors led into the various apartments and rooms, and Ally spotted a woman standing in the breezeway of the open doors, her brightly colored dress unbuttoned down the front, either for air-conditioning or advertising.

Ally heard a loud thud and was knocked backward. Something hit the car and spun it around. She grabbed the handgrip, and Sam cranked the wheel like a race car driver. The tires skidded and burning rubber sent up a cloud of thick black smoke, but Ally's seat belt held her firm.

Just as they came to a shuddering stop, the skies opened and poured raindrops as big as fists. They burst against the car windows, making it impossible to see out. The smell of ozone permeated the air, overpowering even the burnt rubber. They must have had some kind of accident.

"Are you all right?" Sam turned her around and looked her over.

"I'm fine," she said. "Did we hit something?"

"I think we *got* hit. Lightning. It's not safe to stay in this car."

"That was lightning?" Ally looked up at the strangely lit sky, wincing as thunder boomed directly overhead. It was close enough to shake the car. He was right. The rumbling and roaring was deafening. This wasn't safe.

Sam pulled the car to the curb, let himself out and sprinted around to her side. He opened her door, shielding her from the steamy downpour with his body. "We're not far from where I need to go. We'll have to get there on foot."

He helped her out of the car and slammed the door, still trying to protect her from the weather. She hadn't dressed for it, as he'd suggested. She'd worn a sundress and sandals.

"It's a couple blocks. Can you run," he asked her, "or should I carry you?"

Of course, she could run. "Carry me," she said.

THEY WERE BOTH DRENCHED by the time Sam had carried her to his destination. The decaying brick building was oddly quaint with baskets of red geraniums and dark green ivy swaying from the wrought iron balcony and had a leering gargoyle for a door knocker.

The wooden gate gave out an anguished groan as Sam opened it with a slam of his shoulder. Ally felt the jolt run through both their bodies. The door opened onto a court-yard cluttered with more flowers and wrought-iron furniture. Even in a tropical storm, this place looked like a cozy refuge.

"You can put me down now," she said.

He ignored her, of course. But once he had her inside the tiny vestibule that was also a stairwell to the second floor, he set her down.

They were both dripping and pools of water formed at their feet on the gray cement floor. Sam was breathing hard. They clung to each other for several moments, glued by their wet clothing and the ordeal they'd just been through. They could have been killed in the lightning strike, both of them. It was sobering.

The wind turned chilly against Ally's wet clothing. She shivered, and Sam pulled her into his arms, holding her close for a moment. He was as wet as she was but the warmth and support of his body blanketed her, setting off a chain reaction of shivers deliciously mixed with pleasure.

"I have towels upstairs," he said. "Let's go up and dry off."

Ally didn't argue as he took her hand and brought her up the stairs with him. The dimly lit passage had seen better days. Paint was peeling off the walls and the railing was loose. Flashes of lightning alternately lit the way like a floodlight and sank it into darkness. Ally wouldn't have been surprised to see the ghosts of the lovely Creole women who'd displayed themselves on the balconies.

She hurried to keep up with Sam. When they reached the second-floor landing, the hallway wasn't much wider than the stairs. A wooden banister painted black was all that stood between them and a nasty fall to the courtyard below. Other than old-world charm, the rooming house had little to recommend it. She couldn't imagine what Sam wanted with a place like this.

He stopped at the last door and fished a key from his pocket. "It's not much," he said, waving her inside, "but it's safe. We can talk freely in here."

"No bugs?"

He grinned. "Only the eight-legged kind."

"Wonderful."

He opened the door to a cathedral-like room that was breezy from the steamy air blowing through the cracks in the balcony doors. The bathroom was an alcove with a sink and commode separated only by a curtain of shiny dark red beads. A wide arch revealed the bedroom, that had a ghostly white iron bed, draped with mosquito netting next to the rattling balcony doors. The rest of the room was bare except for a long metal table in the kitchenette loaded with electronic equipment.

Sam closed the door to the hallway. Ally smoothed back her dripping hair with her hands as he went to the bathroom for towels.

"The light switch is on your left," he told her.

The room took on a dusty glow when she flipped the switch, reminding her of sunsets she'd seen. A chandelier hung from a ceiling that must have been fifteen feet high.

"I keep my equipment here," he called to her from the bathroom.

She could see that the table held a laptop computer, a tape recorder, some folders and a stack of cassette tapes, both audio and video. There was another piece of equipment that looked like a projector of some kind, and it seemed to have a remote control that went with it. The small kitchenette was neat and tidy. There were a few dishes in the drainer suggesting that he'd eaten meals here.

Sam came through the beaded curtains, his arms piled high with fluffy towels. He handed her two from the top of the pile, took one for himself and set the rest on the chair. He'd already kicked off his shoes and the soles of his feet left moist footprints on the hardwood floor as he strode over to the balcony doors and opened them.

A gust of wind raced into the room flinging the lacy white sheers high into the air. An entire row of them fluttered like the sails of a spinnaker. A beautiful sight, and the breeze was refreshing.

Some fresh air wouldn't hurt this place. At one time it might have been a splendid room. Possibly an artist's loft or even a lovers' rendezvous. Now it looked sadly neglected, although the hardwood floor still had a high polish and the bed was its own ethereal chamber.

As she toweled off, Ally noticed there was no television or sofa, no coffee tables or standing lamps, no plants or pictures. Nothing except Sam's equipment to remind one of modern times. It wouldn't be hard to imagine living a century ago in this place.

Close by lightning struck, the jagged bolt looking as if it might come right through the balcony doors. Ally bit back a gasp as the overhead lights flickered and went out.

Sam rushed over to the metal table and yanked the plug to his extension cord out of the wall. An electrical power surge could have destroyed his equipment. That might be why he'd insisted on coming here—to make sure nothing was damaged.

Another gust blew through the room and Ally shivered. The breeze made her wet clothes as cold as ice.

Sam went to shut the balcony doors. "You should get out of those wet clothes. I have a bathrobe if you want it."

The thought of shucking her wet clothes almost equaled the fantasy of a hot shower but Ally didn't want to be that naked right now. "I'm fine."

A moment later she was sneezing repeatedly. Sam's wry chuckle was sympathetic. "You aren't fine." He disappeared into the bathroom and came back with an indigo blue velour robe.

"It's all yours," he said, nodding toward the room he'd just vacated. "Nobody will look. Not even the bugs."

Ally disappeared behind the beaded curtain to peel off her wet clothing and put on the robe. Once that was done she felt almost human again. Her skin felt tender though, and she wondered if the bruising rain might have caused the sensitivity.

She pulled the robe down over one shoulder and turned to inspect her back in the mirror. She saw no marks anywhere, so she inspected the other side, and then she turned around to have a look at her breasts and her legs.

As she opened the robe's lapel, she heard him clear his throat. He was watching her, despite what he'd said. His reflection in the glass was hard and expressionless, but his eyes were not. They were glimmering with dark urges. Beautiful urges.

She continued what she was doing. With a boldness that was becoming familiar to her around him, she surveyed her chest area, even lifting her breast to look at the underside. It was dangerous, she knew. She couldn't be sure how he might react. His strength made her feel safe, but he was too unpredictable to ever take for granted.

As she touched herself, she wondered if he would come up behind her and put his hands on her. She could almost feel him reaching around and cupping her breasts, and her stomach dipped with pleasure. When she looked up, he was no longer watching her. He'd pulled off his shirt and was toweling himself dry.

He scrubbed his upper body vigorously, bringing a pink glow to his skin. Muscles rippled as he worked. He'd probably left on the wet pants so as not to shock her silly. She was already familiar with his anatomy but not quite bold enough to deal with a full frontal of Sam Sinclair.

She turned to him, embarrassed at how hard her heart was pounding. The storm outside had nothing on her, but she couldn't allow herself to forget what was important here. "Sam?"

She stared at him, on tenterhooks.

"What?" He tilted his head, apparently echoing her question of that morning.

Why was this so difficult? Her throat had all but closed up. "Please get my sister out of there. I don't want her to go through what I did."

The look on his face told her she'd struck a chord. It might have nothing to do with her. Possibly there was some other woman in his life who'd been done wrong by a man, maybe even by him, and the memory of it made him angry. His jaw had turned to stone. His expression was set with disgust.

"I'll get her out. I gave you my word."

"And I believe you." She wasn't reassuring him as much as herself. She really was counting on him—and believing in him—even though it went against her instincts. "Just know this," she said, "I don't care what you have to do to get her out of there. Anything it takes, you have my blessing."

He draped the towel around his neck, silent, gazing back at her as she waited for some response. In the ticking seconds that followed she realized several things. She wanted to be crushed in his arms. Possibly it was their brush with death that made the wanting feel so urgent or maybe it was just the desire to escape from grim reality for awhile. Whatever it was that drove her, she was hope-lessly attracted to him and she needed the consolation of a man's touch, his love, even if only briefly, and even if he didn't love her. Some human closeness.

There was only one thing holding her back. He didn't seem to want that closeness with her. What if he rejected her? That would be devastating.

A clap of thunder shook the doors, but Ally was barely aware of it.

Let well enough alone, she told herself. He's going to get your sister out of there, and that's all you care about. Don't do anything to interfere with that. Don't play with your emotions or his. Don't make complicated what is very simple. He's going to help you. Ignore your own needs, whatever they are. They're not important now. No matter how badly you might want closeness and comfort, you can't do that. You can't—

A flash of lightning blinded her. The doors banged open, blown by a gust of wind. Ally let out the cry that had been trapped inside her for days. She started for Sam but he was there before she could take two steps. She gripped him, shivering and moaning. It wasn't about the storm but he didn't know that.

"Don't let me do anything stupid," she pleaded, looking up at him.

He stared at her for several seconds. Finally, he bent and kissed her on the mouth, a curse burning in his throat. "Shit, I couldn't *get* any more stupid when it comes to you."

She swallowed a sob of relief—and kissed him back. He could not have said anything more perfect. Sometimes she felt like such an idiot around him. He was kissing her the way she'd always dreamed of being kissed. His hands were in her hair, and his mouth moved softly on hers.

She was too absorbed even to wrap her arms around his neck. He made her want all the things that only young girls believed were possible, undying love and total bliss.

Did he really feel stupid around her? What kind of a man would admit that?

A sound slipped out of her, and it must have told him how vulnerable she was because he cupped the back of her head with his palm, holding her spellbound as he thoroughly ravished her mouth. It was the kind of kiss that pushed people over the edge of reason. Ally could so easily imagine it swirling into a passionate tryst in this lovers' hideaway. But Sam didn't let it swirl into anything else. He broke away, almost angrily. "We can't do this."

"I know we can't," she said, "but God, I want to—"

"Want to?" He groaned. "It's insane how much I want you."

"Thank you!"

She hugged him and he stilled. Suddenly he drew back, searching her expression. "You don't have to do this to get your sister back."

"I wasn't thanking you for that." Despair welled inside her as he backed away. God, what a mess this was. Bad idea. This sex stuff was a bad idea. Her eyelids stung with something that could have been tears and she glanced at the door. She had to get out of here. If she was going to break down, at least it wouldn't be in front of him.

"Don't go."

His voice was so low she didn't know how she'd heard it.

"It would kill me if you went now," he said.

He was standing in the wind; the curtains blowing around him. Her legs didn't want to hold her as she walked across the room to him. Rain drenched her, diluting the sting of her tears. She untied her robe and it hit the floor as she stepped into his arms.

Naked. Naked in Sam Sinclair's arms. It felt better than anything had a right to feel. She was flooded with emotions, including guilt that she was giving herself to a near stranger while her sister was in jeopardy, but even that wasn't enough to stop her. Nothing could. Not the rain or the wind or the raging storm. Not even the lightning. She had lost all touch with reality.

The only things that existed were a balcony room and a man and a woman.

Sam fought the doors shut and locked them. When he had that done, he scooped her up in his arms. Somehow by the time he had her on the bed, he'd already joined their bodies.

They were going to make love. No, they *were* making love. Ally felt the power of his thighs forcing her legs apart, the muscled hardness of his body moving inside her. He was hot. Huge. She let out a cry of shock as she was pinned to the bed by his weight.

Suddenly she was uncontrollable. And God, it was sweet. She threw her arms around him, accepting him, embracing him. He was everything she wanted and needed. More than she could handle. Her hands roamed his back, his hips and buttocks, discovering him, feeling the wonder of his body.

A deep thrust brought a cry from her soul. Her fingernails sank into his flanks, and she felt him flinch, but it was pleasure, not pain. He was lost in the bliss of two bodies, throbbing with need. She held him tight, aching because it was that way for her, too.

Pleasure. Such ridiculous pleasure. This was no accident.

He lifted her, rocked her, buried his hands in her hair. They'd fallen into the primal rhythms of mating. But just as she reached for him, he rolled her over and pulled her on top of him. Ally moaned, overwhelmed by the sensation of having him lodged so deeply inside her. They rolled again and he was above her, driving into her, thundering like the storm outside.

Her whole body ached with the joy of it. As she looked into his eyes, she realized that she hadn't lost touch with reality. This was real. They were sharing something precious and honest. She wanted to be here. Wanted this stolen moment of joy.

The emotions amazed her. She touched his face and he lifted her up. Feverishly kissed her. He was as hungry as she was. They were both in the grip of unyielding need, and she'd never known anything as sweet. Her soul had been crying out for this.

"Don't ever regret this," he said. "It's right."

He took her face in his hands, and her heart surged. "Sam, what is this? What's happening? I want to say crazy things like I love you, but we don't even know each other."

His features went through a dizzying series of emotions as he gazed down at her. She saw surprise, disbelief, fear and hot, flaring passion. His feelings were as complex as hers. She was racked with conflict, too. Still, she shouldn't have said it. Embarrassed, she averted her eyes.

"Look at me," he said.

She did, reluctantly, and was surprised at the tenderness she saw.

"We know each other better than you think," he said. "In fact, I know something about you that you don't know yourself."

"What's that?"

"You snore."

"What? I do not!"

"You do. It's a very sweet little snore. You sound like an asthmatic kitten, but it's definitely a snore."

She tried to push him away. Of course, it didn't work. He was buried inside her. "I'm never doing this with you again," she threatened.

"Oh, I think you are. I think you're going to do this with me a lot."

"In your dreams."

"There, too."

He feathered her lips with his mouth—and then he withdrew and made love to her that way, feathering every tender part of her body with his lips. She quivered with pleasure, and when he finally arrived at the cleft of her legs, it was so intense, she cried.

He left her swooning, but he was so unbearably aroused they made love again. Immediately. If he hadn't had a mission to complete, they probably would have continued into the evening, maybe until morning.

Afterward Ally didn't know how to feel about what they'd done. But when Sam opened the doors and she saw the tiniest hint of sunlight peeking through the dark clouds, she told herself it was a sign that they weren't going to be punished for their lapse—and maybe the heavens were celebrating.

Sam's mission tonight would go well. It had to.

# 13

ALLY PICKED at the Chinese chicken salad she'd ordered from room service. Before he left for the club, Sam had insisted she get something. It had been a whirlwind day, and they'd never stopped to eat—never even thought about it. Who could think about food when you were getting hit by lightning…over and over again.

She was still rocked by what they'd done this afternoon—by the feelings and by what a life force of a man Sam was. But she was back to being bewildered by how eagerly they'd both abandoned their concerns. There'd been no time to talk about it afterward. When their own storm was over, they'd had to turn their minds immediately to that evening and Sam's mission at the club.

Sam had gathered up what he needed from his work table—the projector and remote, plus a metal box, the contents of which he wouldn't discuss, saying she was better off not knowing. It bothered her that he didn't seem to trust her enough to share his plans. She hadn't hesitated to tell him how to find the key rooms and passageways in the club—or to share her body with him. But it was also a relief to have something other than the sex to focus on, she had to admit.

She'd felt naked around him afterward, as if she'd been

stripped of her normal emotional protections. It wouldn't have surprised her if he'd felt that way, too. His stupidity remark had suggested that he was vulnerable, that he didn't easily open up about himself.

She speared a piece of chicken and dragged it through the sweet and sour dressing, knowing she wasn't going to eat it. The fork landed on the plate with a clink. With a sigh, she swung around and slipped off the barstool, leaving the salad on the wet bar's granite countertop. She should have been starving, but she was too anxious now to have an appetite. Sam had left over an hour ago, and she'd heard nothing from him since.

An hour wasn't *that* long. It just felt like a lifetime.

That's what she kept telling herself.

She crossed the sitting room to the terrace doors. It was already dark outside, and she couldn't see anything beyond the glittering city lights since it was still steamy and warm from the downpour. The first thing she and Sam had done when they got back to the suite was change out of their wet clothes, which they'd hung in the shower on a retractable line.

Sam had put on a tux for his night at the club, and she'd put on silk cami-pajamas, possibly trying to convince herself that she would lie around and watch TV while he rescued her sister. That hadn't worked, of course. Her racing mind seemed to be propelling her feet, and she couldn't sit still.

Worse, she was getting paranoid.

Getting? If paranoia were money, she'd be stinking rich. She'd gone back to asking herself if this afternoon had been a terrible mistake, and she was going to be punished for it. She couldn't bear to think that her impulsive behavior might have made things worse for Vix.

"Reckless behavior," she said on a tight sigh. She *had* been reckless, even in the way she picked out Sam and tried to blackmail him into helping her. Desperation had driven her, but that didn't explain this afternoon. She had not had sex with him to thank him. It had felt as if she'd been born to be naked in his arms. She'd wanted it— and he'd resisted up until the very last. In a way, she'd seduced him.

"Great," she said, wondering what else she could add to her list of crimes. She still hadn't told him about the second e-mail from Vix. She was afraid he would back out of their agreement. Vix was eighteen and legally an adult. She could make her own decisions. But should Sam have been trusted with that information?

Ally couldn't think about this anymore. There didn't seem to be any right answers. She closed the terrace doors and headed for the bedroom. She was going to get in bed, turn on the TV and read the crawl on CNN. Anything to distract herself. The self-recrimination was pointless now even if deserved.

But it was too hot to get under the covers, so she flopped around on top, staring like a zombie at the flat-panel television screen hanging on the opposite wall. She could have turned on the air and shut the bedroom doors, which also opened to the terrace, but she felt closed in as it was.

Nothing seemed to ease her anxiety. She flipped through a couple dozen stations looking for anything that would take her mind off what was happening at the club and ended up at the Weather Channel where they were talking about that day's thunderstorm—the *last* thing she wanted to think about. At some point later, she went in search of the morning paper, desperate enough to try the crossword puzzle despite her love-hate relationship with crosswords. In her experience they were rigged with trick clues that only puzzle insiders knew, and they made her feel dumb.

Now she was sitting in the overstuffed chair near the terrace doors, flipping through visitor information books. She'd started a feature on hot new local restaurants ten times but couldn't get past the first paragraph. And it was only ten o'clock, an hour since she'd come to the bedroom, two hours since Sam left. She got up from the chair and went to the bathroom, thinking she'd seen some shiny new women's magazines next to the wicker basket of toiletries. As she entered the room, the line of wet clothing caught her eye, and she took a moment to see if any of it was dry. She hesitated at Sam's jacket. The canvas fabric was still damp, but that wasn't what had stopped her. She was just now remembering that he'd stuffed the torn pages from the book inside his jacket.

They were wadded up in an inner pocket, as if he'd meant to throw them away, not save them. She carefully smoothed them with her hands on the marble countertop. The page displayed an extensive family tree. The descendant named on the very last branch was Samuel Micha Wolverton. Based on his birthdate, he was thirty-eight, unmarried, and the only surviving Wolverton except for a paternal uncle and his wife, who were childless.

The family tree went back several generations and took up the entire page. The other page displayed old family photos with captions that were small and difficult to read because of the wrinkling. Ally didn't understand how the Wolverton family history had anything to do with Jason

Aragon and his alleged criminal activities. Or why Sam would want copies of either page badly enough to deface public property.

She went over each photograph, getting close enough to read the captions. "Sam?" she whispered as she came to a photo of Samuel Micha Wolverton. It was taken twenty years ago on his eighteenth birthday, and he was wearing a military uniform, possibly about to ship out somewhere. A dozen or so members of his family were in the picture but he was at the center of the group. Ally recognized him immediately.

Samuel M. Wolverton was a young Sam Sinclair.

The man's height, his dark gold hair and unwavering stare were all Sam's. And they were Micha's features, too. Now Ally understood her feeling of déjà vu the first time she'd seen him up close. She'd come across a picture of Micha, Sam's great-grandfather, all those years ago when the lower level was under construction, and she'd been held hostage down there.

Jason's safe room had originally been a storage room, and she'd found a trunk full of odds and ends, including rolled canvases that were old family portraits. They'd been portraits of Wolverton ancestors, including Micha. His was the image that had come into her head when she'd dreamed of the ghost in the graveyard, and then moments later, when she'd seen Sam, face-to-face.

Ally's breath came out in a low, shaky whistle. She could hardly believe what she'd found. At least now she could stop blaming herself for everything. She wasn't the only one keeping secrets. It appeared Sam had his own agenda, one that involved the Wolvertons and had nothing to do with a Treasury Department money-laundering case. She wondered if he'd been lying about everything.

Her heart began to race as she stared at her reflection in the mirror. She had a big evening ahead of her. And she would have to dress very carefully for the occasion. She'd already worn the lace dress, so it would have to be the pink champagne chiffon, possibly with her hair piled high on her head. That should go nicely with her stiletto sandals, beaded bag and the mask with its sexy black cockatiel feathers.

She was going to Club Casablanca, and she'd already figured out how to get past the security guard at the door. Jason…well, he was another matter. He was due back tonight, and she would have to be very sure that she wasn't recognized. Regardless she had quite a surprise in store for Sam Sinclair.

"I'M HERE FOR Sam Sinclair," Ally told the security guard who stopped her in the club's anteroom. "He's expecting me."

She'd already decided if the guard didn't stop her she would walk straight into the club. She wanted to look that sure of her right to enter Jason Aragon's private enclave.

"I'll need to see your ID," the guard told Ally. She wasn't the woman who'd frisked Ally but she was a perfect security guard for this place—beautiful, unsmiling and icy.

Ally flashed her a dazzling smile. "That won't be necessary," she said, raising her voice to signal that she had nothing to hide—and more importantly, wasn't opposed to creating a scene. "Just page Mr. Sinclair, if you would. He'll identify me. Tell him that Rosalyn Wolverton Sims is here.

"Do it," Ally added, her voice now soft and menacing.

The guard looked wary but did as Ally asked. Ally had pulled rank. A security guard couldn't take the chance of offending the guest of a VIP platinum key member.

Ally began counting the seconds. It took Sam less than twenty to get there. And he was angry. She could see the low blaze in his eyes but she wasn't surprised that he'd been prompt. Hoping to get his attention, she'd taken the name of one of his great aunts from his family tree. She had no idea what he had to lose in this game he was playing. For her it was everything.

"Sam, tell this woman I'm Rosie, your second cousin twice removed," she said, laughing and winking. "She thinks I'm trying to crash the party."

Just moments later they were inside the club, and Sam was pulling her into an alcove to speak with her privately. Or possibly she was pulling him. Either way, they were in each other's faces.

"What are you doing here?" He gripped her wrist as if she might try to escape him. "And who the hell are you supposed to be?"

She raised an eyebrow. "Samuel Micha Wolverton doesn't recognize his own great aunt? Maybe I should ask who *you're* supposed to be."

His eyes narrowed to a dangerous gleam, and Ally felt a shiver of fear. Possibly he had a great deal to lose? She couldn't tell if he remembered leaving the crumpled pages in his coat but he clearly wasn't admitting to anything. Any thought of trying to coerce information out of him was quickly abandoned. She wasn't that reckless, and they were already getting some inquisitive looks from patrons of the club. Ally didn't want to be locked in mortal combat with him if Angelic showed up.

"Put your mask on," Sam ordered under his breath. Apparently he could read minds *and* body language.

Ally had looped the cockatiel mask around the strap of her evening bag. She wasted no time getting the mask on—and immediately felt less exposed.

"You can't stay," he told her. "It's too dangerous. I can't protect you *and* get your sister out of here."

"Tell me what the plan is. I'll help."

"The way you can help is to *leave*," he said. "We'll go to the bar and have a drink. Then you'll complain of a headache and excuse yourself. No more discussion."

"Why won't you tell me the plan?"

"Think of it as me protecting you. If you knew the plan, Jason could torture it out of you."

"Is Jason here?" She peeked around Sam, checking out the part of the club that she could see.

He moved and blocked her view. "His flight's been delayed because of poor weather conditions according to Angelic. Still, he could charter a plane and show up at any time."

"Then let's go now." She met his perturbed gaze head-on. "Sam, since you won't tell me why you're really here and you won't tell me your plan, you can't expect me to trust you. I'm going down there with you."

"You're leaving."

"I have proof that you're not Sam Sinclair. Don't make me use it."

He drew a deep breath, though his features registered no surprise. He must have been expecting her to make the threat and that concerned her. Did he have some kind of retaliation in mind? Was that why he was so cool? She'd just played her trump card, and it was all she had. He was a seasoned gambler, used to bluffing and being bluffed. There was no way to know what he would do next.

ALLY STOOD in the luxurious ladies' waiting room, looking over her shoulder at her nearly backless gown in the floor-to-ceiling mirror. She'd been so amazed that Sam had finally relented and brought her down to the lower level that she'd come straight here, to the ladies' room to gather her wits.

She wasn't sure what had changed his mind, probably the realization that she wasn't going to change hers, and that he would create an embarrassing scene if he called the security guards or tried to remove her himself. Of course, she would have preferred that he gratefully accept her help. But there'd been nothing grateful about the way he'd insinuated his powerful arm around her waist and escorted her to the elevator. She'd trotted along, listening to his murmured instructions and agreeing to everything, which was essentially to take her cues from him, and to say nothing and do nothing beyond the girlfriend role they'd agreed upon.

Now she was here, part of his plan, whatever that was— and this was their last shot at finding Vix. Sam had said he would scope out the casino area while she was in the ladies' room. She also knew he was waiting until exactly the right moment to enter the maze. Apparently there was a diversion planned. He'd told her that much.

Ally turned to the glass and took one last look at herself, wondering if she was up to the challenge of tonight. The dress and mask made her look like an exotic winged creature capable of anything. Could she really fool Jason if he showed up? Her best bet was to keep a low profile, but at the same time be convincing with Sam, which meant doing the sex kitten thing and fawning all over him. She doubted he'd be very thrilled with that kind of attention tonight. He probably wanted to drown this particular kitten.

She had to admit that his restraint was amazing. Other than the balcony room, which almost felt like a dream now, he hadn't weakened at all, no matter how much she'd tested him. It was one of the reasons she'd been so bold with him. He was the one drawing the line, saying no. But she couldn't be at cross-purposes with him now. She had to cooperate in every way.

As she came out of the waiting room, she saw a man in the shallow alcove of one of the guest rooms across the way smoothing the hang of his tuxedo jacket. He'd been in the elevator with Ally and Sam on their way down, and she'd recognized him. He was Abel Belen, a billionaire European financier who was one of the club's most prestigious members. He was also one of Jason's business partners and a member of the Inner Circle.

Fortunately he didn't seem to recognize her. Belen was as perfectly groomed as Ally remembered, a perfect gentleman in every way—except the way he was looking at her right now.

His gaze followed the curves of her body. Undressing her with his eyes? If she'd been wearing a blouse, he would have been ripping off the buttons.

Ally wasn't going to take the chance of offending him no matter what he did. She smiled back as if she hadn't even noticed his crude behavior. He made a lewd gesture, beckoning her to join him in the alcove.

"Oops, forgot something," she said, ducking back inside the ladies' room door.

He was gone when she came out, and she hurried back to the casino to find Sam. For a moment she had a horrible feeling that something had gone wrong, then she spotted Sam in the high-stakes area at the craps table. It surprised her when he turned, as if he'd sensed her coming, and she walked straight into his arms, showering his unsmiling face with kisses.

"Darling," she murmured, "I don't like to leave you even long enough to freshen up." In his ear she whispered, "Come to the bar with me. I need to talk to you."

He gave her a warning look. That obviously wasn't in his plan.

From behind him, someone tapped on his shoulder, and Sam turned, pulling Ally with him. It was Abel Belen, and his mouth curved into a soft sneer when he saw Ally.

"Your lady has a nice smile," he said. "We met in the hallway a few minutes ago, and I think she's as hot for me as I am for her." He gave Sam a hearty slap on the arm. "I'm challenging you for her."

Sam's fingers dug into the small of Ally's back. "That isn't a good idea," he told the man, his voice barely audible.

The challenger snorted. "What do you mean, old man?" he said, suddenly brusque and loud. "You can't refuse a challenge. It isn't done."

Ally didn't know quite what to do. She was too stunned to protest, and wouldn't have dared anyway. Challenge matches were the highest form of entertainment down here. That's what she warned Sam about, that there was the danger of him being challenged. If he didn't win the match, their plan was ruined. And it was her fault.

# 14

"LET'S GET THIS OVER WITH," Sam said. He released her and grabbed Belen by the arm. Ally wobbled on her stiletto heels as Sam marched the startled man over to the nearest unoccupied card table.

"High card wins," Sam growled to the dealer. "This asshole draws first."

Ally said a silent prayer. This was not how things were done at Club Casablanca. Sam was out of control, and under any other circumstances, she might have found that ironic. And he'd been worried about her?

She crept up behind him and gave him a pinch. He didn't have much in the way of love handles, but there was enough. It wasn't necessary to say anything. He looked her way, and she gave him a warning glare.

*Do not blow this, Sam.*

Belen drew a queen of spades—and was very pleased with himself. He winked at Ally, who controlled herself admirably. She didn't flip him off.

Sam drew a card and waited a beat, as if he were willing it to be a face card, a king.

Ally twisted her evening bag into knots as he turned the card over. He'd drawn a queen as well, but it was hearts. Spades was the higher suit!

Sam crushed the card in his hand. Belen was declared the winner. Ally couldn't believe it was over and Sam had lost.

The crowd applauded, and Belen roared with laugher. He cooed to Ally, "Come to daddy, baby."

Sam flinched as if he'd been hit. His hands curled into fists.

Ally could see there was going to be trouble. "I need a word with Mr. Sinclair," she told the challenger, the dealer and everyone else who was watching, which was the entire room at that point. "We'll just be a minute," she promised.

This wasn't how things were done at Club Casablanca. She tugged Sam away from the gambling tables and the avidly curious looks. When they were out of earshot, she said, "Listen carefully. I remember Belen from before. He's one of Jason's Inner Circle, which could work in our favor. I'll ask Belen to take me to the Moroccan Suite. It's reserved for Jason when he's here, but I'm sure they'd make it available to Belen."

Sam didn't let her finish. "You *want* to be with this guy?"

"No! Let me finish. The Moroccan Suite's in the maze—" She hesitated, trying to remember. "Outside corner, northeast wall, I think. Anyway, I told you about the passageway from the suite's dressing room to the safe room. I can excuse myself to freshen up and check out the safe room myself. If Vix is there, I'll send you a text message."

"You're sure about this passageway?"

"I didn't have a chance to check it out, but I know Jason intended to preserve the passageways that were part of the original house."

She couldn't be sure it still existed, but getting to the

suite was one way to find out. "I have to do this, Sam. It could be our best shot. You asked me to trust you. Now, you have to trust me."

"It's that asshole Belen I don't trust. I don't want you alone with him. What if he—"

"He won't have a chance. Keep checking your phone. When you get my text message, you'll know what to do."

"Christ, Ally. Do you know what you're asking?" His jaw was white at the edges. The sinew in his neck was taut. He looked completely capable of mopping up the place and whisking her out the tunnel to safety. She wouldn't have been surprised if he was armed in some way for a mission like this. He was actually more intimidating than Abel Belen.

But that made her all the more sure that with Sam for backup, she could do this. "They're waiting," she told him. "They're watching us. I need an answer."

SAM SCRATCHED his card against the green felt. "Hit me."

The dealer threw down an ace. Sam flipped the card in his hand. A king. "Blackjack."

The dealer pushed two stacks of one-hundred-dollar chips his way. Sam had no reaction except to stare grimly at the money. *Now* he got the king?

Belen was at the next table, close enough that Sam could hear everything the sick bastard was saying to his fellow players about having a hot time with his prize in the Moroccan Suite, which apparently he'd had no trouble arranging.

Escorted by a security guard, Ally had already left for the suite. She'd flirted outrageously with Belen, telling him she would need time alone to get ready for "daddy"—

and the wait would be worth it. All the while she'd been talking to him, she'd run her little finger along the low-cut neckline of her dress, caressing her breasts. Belen had practically drooled.

Sam had just barely managed to curb his snarl reflex. He didn't believe Ally knew what she was getting into, and he was damn certain she couldn't take care of herself with a pervert like Belen. But Sam's hands had been tied. If he hadn't gone along with her plan, he would have been forced to take on Belen and every security guard in the place. And that would have been the end of his plan to find her sister—and evidence against Aragon.

Sam had begun gambling then, aware that the curious were still watching his reactions, and itching for some excitement. They were going to get some, but later. And he would deal with Belen later, too. Emergency castration without benefit of anesthesia sounded like fun.

As Belen got up to leave, Sam looked at his watch. Twenty minutes had passed since Ally left. If there was an accessible passageway, she may have had time to use it by now. He pulled out his cell and checked it for text messages, but there weren't any.

Had he hit the wrong buttons? He checked again. Nothing.

It was an effort to take his next breath, as if something cold and solid had hit his chest. Fear. He was scared shitless that something had happened to her. Maybe she hadn't been able to get rid of the security guard or he'd come back and caught her in the passageway.

But fear of any kind was the worst thing that could happen to Sam right now. He'd already made all the mistakes he could afford tonight. The security people were watching him like hawks, and he had to find some way to get to the conduit without being seen.

The safest move was probably to go to the bar for a drink, grumble a bit about his losing and tell the bartender he was leaving for the night. Then he could slip into the men's lounge and find the conduit that would take him to the maze. From that point, he would have to hope Ally's directions were good.

"Are you in or out, sir?" the dealer asked.

Sam checked his cell. Still no message.

"Out," he said, picking up his chips.

SAM STOOD in the middle of the marble and mahogany lounge, surveying the place one last time. There was no passageway in here. He'd been over the place from floor to ceiling. He'd even checked the bathroom stalls. Either Ally had steered him wrong—and he couldn't imagine why she'd do that—or she'd been off in her directions.

He'd been lucky no one was using the lounge at this time of night, but he still had to find the passageway. On his way here he'd noticed another door on the hallway that said Employees Only and was key-locked, making it relatively easy to break into.

A furnace room, Sam discovered just moments later, as he stepped into a dark, musty area not much bigger than a large walk-in closet. It housed the mansion's heating and air-conditioning units. In her haste, Ally must have counted the doors wrong.

He found the conduit within minutes. It was an aluminum panel that had been made to look like part of the ventilation system, but was actually a narrow pocket door that had rusted shut from years of not being used.

Sam carried a Swiss Army knife. It didn't take him long to pry the panel loose. When he checked his watch, he saw that Ally had been with Belen nearly an hour. Sam still hadn't received a text message from her. He couldn't wait any longer. He was going in.

THE PASSAGEWAY was dark and cramped, forcing Sam to hunch down to avoid hitting his head. It exited into an empty room that looked about the size of a small interior office. As Sam slapped the dust off his clothes, he realized that he'd come through an opening disguised as a fireplace. Not terribly creative, but how many places had passageways these days.

He mentally repeated Ally's directions in his head as he let himself out of the room and scanned the hallway, determining which way to go.

*Outside corner, northeast wall.*

After one false start, he reversed directions and two hallways later, found himself at intricately carved double doors with a plaque on the wall that said Moroccan Suite. The doors weren't locked, and he immediately suspected a trap. When he pushed one of them open, he saw a man lying prone on the floor. It was Abel Belen, and Ally was struggling to flip him over onto his back.

Sam entered the room and shut the door. "What happened to him?"

"I don't know." Ally looked near tears. "I talked him into having a massage, and he blacked out."

"Why didn't you send me a message?"

"And let him suffocate? Help me turn him over. Somebody has to give him mouth-to-mouth."

Sam grimaced. "It's not going to be me—and it's not going to be you, either."

She continued to struggle with Belen's dead weight, so Sam knelt to help her. As they turned him over, something that looked like a credit card fell out of one of his pockets. Sam ignored it, assuming it was a player's card that calculated credits earned for gambling. He concentrated on checking the man's pulse and taking his respiration. Both were slow but steady.

"He's breathing," Sam assured her. "He's just out cold. How the hell did you manage that?"

"I'm not sure. I read an article once on pulse point massage. It said there was a myth about a point behind the ear that could knock you out if you hit it just right. I guess it's not a myth."

"Guess *not*. We need to talk," Sam said as he went to lock the doors. Ally was on her feet by the time he got back to her. "Did you find the passageway to the safe room?"

"Yes, but Vix isn't there. And it doesn't look like anybody's been there in months, maybe years. The dust is thick."

Now he understood the distress in her expression. It wasn't for Belen. It was for her sister.

"Let's get out of here," Sam said. "You're going back to the hotel."

"No! We have to check out the rest of the maze."

"*I'll* check out the rest of the maze." He was harsh, emphatic. "You wanted the plan. Here it is. As soon as I leave this suite, you call the security guards. Tell them Belen blacked out on you and you have no idea why.

Insist on going upstairs with him. Say you want to be there when the paramedics arrive. I'm assuming you drove your car here, so once you're upstairs you can make an excuse and duck out."

She was shaking her head, but he plunged on, not giving her a chance. He wanted her to be overwhelmed, to go along with him. There wasn't time for anything else. "I'll text message you when I've found her, Ally."

"Sam, let me look for her with you."

He stabbed a finger at the man on the floor. "We can't leave Belen like this. You were the last one seen with him. They'll come after you, Ally, and since you're supposed to be my girlfriend, the first place they'll look is my hotel suite."

She pressed her hand to her mouth. Her face was pale and tense.

"Ally, we have to move. Jason's due any time."

"All right." A slight nod, but she looked torn.

"Can you do this?" Sam asked.

She took a wobbly step, and he knew she wasn't okay. He pulled her into his arms, holding her, supporting her and wishing he could give her what she so desperately wanted—her sister back, safe.

She sighed in defeat, and his heart wrenched.

"Okay, let's go look for her." He sucked in a breath, resolving himself. "We'll do it together. When we've found her, I'll initiate my diversion and we'll all get out of here."

She looked up at him, astonished. "But, what about your mission? How are you going to get Jason?"

"If I can't get him, someone else will have to." She'd already figured out that he wasn't here just to bust Jason Aragon. It was personal—and maybe the only thing he'd ever done in his life that would count as selfless. But he couldn't explain any of that to her now.

"You would do that?" she said.

She winced, as if she might be on the verge of breaking down, but Sam couldn't let that happen. "Come on," he said, taking her hand. "Let's go find her."

She let go of his hand and pushed him away. "Go," she said. "*Go,* I trust you."

ALLY LEFT HER RENTAL CAR in the self-parking area of the Lafayette, locked it and then broke into a run toward the back entrance of the hotel. She couldn't just walk. A coil of aching tension propelled her. She'd had doubts all the way back about whether she'd done the right thing. It had felt as if she'd abandoned Vix, and if anything happened—

Ally killed the idea with an obscene word. Her own mind had become the enemy. The only thing she could control right now was her thoughts, which meant she had to challenge the doubts or they would paralyze her. She needed to be ready for anything, ready in case Sam called. Or the authorities showed up.

The paramedics had quickly revived Belen, but he'd refused to be taken to the hospital. He'd blamed the blackout on having too much to drink, and he'd never mentioned Ally's massage, to her great relief. Apparently he didn't want to discuss the situation with the paramedics.

Ally had taken Sam's advice and quietly ducked out the second she knew Belen was going to be all right, but not without concerns that he might change his mind and have her charged with assault, if he realized it was her massage that had knocked him out. He was a powerful man, who could easily take action against her—or insist that Jason do it.

At least she'd gotten out of the club before Jason showed up.

The hotel's halls were empty as she made her way to the same elevator she'd used the first time she'd gone up to Sam's room. There'd been a lot on the line that time, too, but nothing like this.

When she got to the suite, she fished her key card from her bag and slid the card into the slot. Nothing happened. She tried it again. The card didn't work? She was already paranoid, and now questions exploded in her head. Had she been locked out of the room? Were they after her already?

She took a look at the card, wondering if she'd inserted it wrong. It wasn't the hotel's card, she saw immediately. This was the one that had fallen out of Belen's jacket. She'd slipped it into her purse, thinking it was a room key that might come in handy in some way. It had an odd holographic design that resembled computer circuitry. From different angles, the images changed, disappearing and reappearing.

Ally had never seen anything quite like it before, but her thoughts were too jumbled to try and figure out what it might be. She returned it to her purse and continued digging until she found the key card.

This time the door opened. But the sounds of people talking made her hesitate. Someone was in the room.

Ally crept into the narrow foyer, but she could only see through to the terrace doors, which were open. She definitely hadn't left them that way. It sounded like the TV was playing. As she drew closer, she realized there were two people sitting on the sitting room sofa, a man and a woman, apparently engrossed in whatever was on the screen.

They were looking the other way, but as the woman turned to speak to the man, Ally saw her face and recognized her. She recognized them both.

Ceramic beads made a terrible clatter as Ally's bag hit the marble floor. "Oh, my God," she whispered.

# 15

"VICTORIA?" Ally spoke her sister's name softly, not quite trusting her eyes. The tall, auburn-haired beauty who had just sprung up from the couch couldn't be her baby sister, could it?

"Ally, I'm sorry—" Vix hung back, as if afraid of what Ally might say or do. The young man who rose protectively and stood behind her was Mike Stiles, the rock musician boyfriend that Ally didn't approve of and had asked Vix not to see.

"How did you get away from Jason?" Ally asked her. "Did Mike help you? Why didn't you e-mail me and tell me what was going on?"

Vix pulled and twisted a long tendril of her chestnut-gold hair. Her green eyes were so big and vulnerable that she looked more like a twelve-year-old than the eighteen-year-old she now was. Not that she'd ever let anyone forget her adult status, especially Ally.

"Promise you won't be mad?" Vix said.

She looked utterly miserable standing there, like a kid caught sneaking in after curfew. She tried to laugh, but cried instead. How many times had they played out this exact scene? It was definitely her sister.

"Are you all right? Tell me what happened." Ally started toward her, but Vix waved her hand frantically.

"Wait, stay there. Promise first. Promise you won't be angry."

"All right, I promise! Vix, do you know how frightened I've been? Sam's at the club now, searching for you."

The hair-twisting stopped. "Who's Sam?" Vix was suddenly suspicious. "And why would he be searching for me?"

How to explain Sam? Ally had been masquerading for so long it was hard to remember the basics. "He's a member of Jason's club, and I made a bargain with him. I promised to provide him with certain information if he would get me into the club and help me find you."

"Information about what?"

"That's not something we need to talk about right now," Ally said, which seemed to make Vix even more suspicious.

"So, this Sam is a friend of yours?"

"Not exactly."

Vix picked up one of the tasseled satin-and-velvet pillows from the couch as if it were evidence. "This has to be his suite, right? You could never afford it. The chambermaid let us in, by the way. The one you talked about in your e-mail."

Ally had responded to Vix's last message, urging her to call or come to the Lafayette Hotel. Ally had given her the chambermaid's name in case she wasn't there.

Vix continued looking around. "Are you staying here with him, Sam?"

"Well, yes, but it's just for appearances. We're not actually—"

The pillow slipped from her fingers. "Holy shit, are you sleeping with him?"

"Watch the language," Ally warned.

"You sound like my mother, which *you're* not."

Ally threw up her hands. "Enough of this! I'm not the one who's been missing for days. Would you please answer my question? How did you get out of the club?"

Vix chewed on her lip and looked at her boyfriend. "I was never in the club," she said in a small voice. "Mike and I were going to run away together. We were going to disappear, and we made up the Jason thing to throw you off track."

"Run away? You were never being held in the club?"

Vix hung her head. Her boyfriend encircled her with his arms, and she pressed against him, as if she were trying to disappear now. "I figured you'd believe me if I said I was being held at the club," she explained, "because it had happened to you."

"We had to do it." Mike cleared his throat and stood tall. "You totally freaked when Victoria told you the truth, that she and I wanted to get married. You threatened to call her mom and dad—and my parents, too."

"I didn't *threaten*. I suggested to her that we should all discuss it."

Vix flared. "You threatened—and what is there to discuss? It's my life, and I'm old enough to make my own decisions."

Mike gripped Vix's shoulders, supporting her. He nodded his agreement. Watching him, Ally realized what she must have feared the most. He cared about Vix as much as her sister did him. She'd never questioned the intensity of her sister's feelings for Mike, just the rationality of them. Now she knew it was mutual.

Ally's heart twisted. They were too young. Love could

hurt like hell, and nothing could protect them from it now. She really didn't know quite what to say to them, but she had made a mistake by trying to stop them from seeing each other. They were bonded—and desperate.

"What you did was wrong," she said, "but I understand why you did it."

Vix sighed, contrite, but impatient. "That's why we're here now, to talk to you about our future. We want to be together."

"I know," Ally assured her, "and we will talk, but there's something I have to do first."

"What?" Vix seemed astonished that anything could come before her urgent considerations.

Ally dug through her evening bag in search of her cell phone. As she pulled things out of the zipper compartment, a tube of lipstick dropped to the floor, along with a packet of tissues and the card that Belen had been carrying. She didn't bother to pick anything up. She was in too much of a hurry.

"Ally, *what* are you doing?"

Ally quelled her sister with a glance. "Victoria, there's a man who's risking his life to find you tonight, and somehow I have to let him know that you're all right. I've already botched things badly and if anything happens to him, I'll never forgive—"

Ally broke off, startled at herself. Talk about intense. She found the phone, flipped it open and began to tap out a text message to Sam, praying he'd left his cell on vibrate.

vix is safe, she typed. at hotel w/me. where r u?

Just seconds later, her cell began to vibrate, and the text message signal appeared on her screen. She hit a button to bring it up.

in vault, the message read. cant crack system. takes pass card.

He was in the Vault, but he couldn't crack the computer system.

Sweat broke out on Ally's temples. She dropped to the floor in a crouch and picked up the card. Her hand began to shake as she realized that this could be the card Sam needed. Belen was a member of the Inner Circle and would have had that kind of access to the computer system. She had to go back to the club.

She slipped the card in her bra. Still crouched on the floor, she started another message to Sam.

i have pass card, she typed. how do i get to u?

Before he could respond, Ally felt a hand on her shoulder. Her sister was peering down at her, concern in her eyes.

"Ally, what's going on? Are you okay?"

Ally lied through her teeth. "Of course! I'm fine. You guys will be all right here for a bit, won't you?" she said. "I have to deliver something. It's important."

"Where are you going? Do you need help?"

"I have to get to Sam. No more questions, please."

Vix whistled softly. "Wow, whoever this Sam guy is, you've got it bad."

"What?" Ally shot Vix a warning glare. "Don't be ridiculous. I'm just concerned for his safety."

But not a second later, Ally was glued to the phone's display, waiting for another message, praying for another message.

U MUST DO what i say. don't want u hurt.

It was Sam's last text message before he'd typed out a string of instructions that would get Ally into the club in a very unusual way. But even more unusual was what he told her to wear—and do. She was going to be his diversion.

She'd followed his instructions to the letter. There hadn't been time to do anything else. Vix and Mike had helped her get dressed and ready. When she'd made them understand that Sam's life was at stake, they'd stopped asking questions and come to her aid.

Now she was on her way to the club, driving as fast as she dared, and repeating the rest of Sam's instructions in her head. He'd stressed that she must follow them step by step—and how dangerous it would be if she didn't.

SAM STOOD at the end of the bar, turning an empty shot glass in his fingers. He hadn't even tasted the fifty-year-old whiskey, much less felt its effects. Tonight he could have had ten drinks and not been affected. His adrenaline was off the scale.

He'd come back to the casino to wait for Ally's signal. The diversion would be in the high-stakes area, which was deserted now and should stay that way for the next fifteen minutes or so. Every night at ten, the hostesses staged a bawdy little song-and-dance number on a revolving stage in the middle of the casino. Tonight that dance was Sam's window of opportunity. The stage was far enough away from the high-stakes tables that no one would get hurt, especially Ally.

His gut twisted at the thought. He'd allowed her to help only because he'd known that she considered last night's fiasco her fault, and one way or another she was determined to get the pass card to him. If she was going to take that kind of risk, he wanted to walk her through it, and she had shown up at exactly the right time. Not only was he locked out of the computer system, but the lightning storm had damaged the equipment he needed for the diversion—and forced him to come up with another plan.

The bartender glanced Sam's way. Sam shook his head and pushed the shot glass away. There was still no sign of Jason, which was just as well. He might be the only one in this establishment who would know how to deal with the diversion Sam had in mind. Angelic had been in the casino moments ago, but only briefly to meet and greet. Then she'd floated off to fulfill her other duties. It didn't really matter where she was at this point.

Sam's cell was in his breast pocket, set to vibrate. He had a miniature remote control in the palm of his free hand, poised. If Ally had followed his instructions, he would be using the remote momentarily.

He'd barely completed the thought before the cell began to buzz. Everything inside him went still. He left the bar and walked into the casino to make sure the high stakes area was still clear. It was. As he pressed the button he had that moment of thinking there'd been a disconnect, that nothing would happen. He counted the seconds of silence. Just ten? It seemed like an eternity.

It started with a low rumble, as deep as an earthquake. The walls began to shake and the floor rippled like water. The dancers stopped, and the crowd looked around, confused. No one really moved until the noise erupted. Great howling wails of anguish. They came from the walls, the ceiling, the floors—piercing cries that chilled the blood.

People scrambled, ducking under tables and running for the doors. Once they'd found cover, Sam pressed a second button and the wall behind the gaming tables exploded as if it had been hit with a wrecking ball.

There was a sealed tunnel behind the high-stakes area, and Sam had just blown the door. Lights sizzled and popped, bursting like fireworks. The casino went dark and icy air whipped through the room. Even Sam found himself shivering—and he knew exactly how the movie-like special effects had been created.

He'd concealed slender, wireless CD players in the backlit recesses behind the casino's artwork and he'd counted on the prerecorded noises to be greatly enhanced by the lower level's unusual acoustics. For the sealed door, he'd used simple plastique explosives, strategically placed in the tunnel. And the blast of cold air had come from the tunnel itself. Thank God, it had all worked. So far.

As the dust cleared, a luminous white figure could be seen in the gaping hole where the door had been. It seemed to hover in midair, a wraith with robed arms lifted toward the heavens and red eyes, glowing like hot coals.

The howling rose to deafening levels. It was malevolent and triumphant. Everyone who'd heard the ghost stories probably thought they understood what it meant. Micha Wolverton had finally found his way back into The Willows.

Except that it wasn't Micha. That would become clear to anyone who was still watching as the apparition glided into the room. It appeared to be a woman in a gown as wispy as cirrus clouds. A hooded cape concealed her, gleaming like white satin.

"The White Rose," a man said as he brushed past Sam on his way out of the bar.

Exactly, Sam thought. The White Rose had found a way

to let her husband back into their home—and put an end to their tragic ghost story. That's what Sam wanted everyone to think.

It was too dark for Sam to see the people leaving the room, but he could hear the stampede. Monique, the elevator Nazi, must have her hands full by now, he thought ironically. He turned on his penlight and made his way across the casino toward the gaming tables—and the ghost.

She was emitting the only significant light in the room, but he happened to know it was coming from the beam of a projector in the tunnel behind her.

Sam pressed the remote one last time, and the projector went out, plunging the lower level in darkness. Now Sam's pen gave out the only light, a tiny ray that hit the White Rose's satin cape and bounced back like a laser light show. Not what Sam had intended. He wanted her concealed, not exposed.

"Lose the cape," Sam whispered as he got close enough to grip her hand. "Hurry up! Let's go!"

ALLY WAS PANTING for breath by the time she and Sam reached the Vault. It hadn't been necessary to go through the passageway. The security guards had fled their post, leaving the entrance unprotected.

Sam released her hand and pressed his palm to the biometric screen on the wall next to the Vault's door. "Thank God," she whispered as the seal popped and the door slid open. Sam had warned her that the club's security system might lock down the Vault and any other vital areas, permitting no one to enter. Evidently, Jason's state-of-the-art system had some flaws.

The room they entered was blindingly bright and freezing cold. Ally clutched herself for warmth—and to hide her sheer negligee. One wall had monitors with major countries and time zones. Another had stock market updates from around the world. It looked like a minifinancial center, and the whirring sounds made Ally wonder if a backup generator was supplying the power.

"What's that?" she asked, pointing to what looked like the door to a closet. Thumping noises shook the walls.

"The night-shift guy," Sam said. "The room is manned 24/7, so I had to deal with him. Looks like he came to."

Sam gestured toward the bank of computers. "I need the pass card. We don't have much time."

Ally dipped her hand into the lace bodice of her nightgown and pulled out the card. Sam didn't smile as he took it, but the glint in his eye told her the thought had crossed his mind. She wore the gown she'd picked out when they'd gone shopping together—the one that had seemed oddly out of place with its classic empire lines and the long flowing layers of silk chiffon. The satin cape had been Vix's idea, and she'd manufactured it from the suite's bedsheets.

Sam went to the nearest computer station and inserted the card. Ally stayed where she was, keeping her eye on the door and the clock. They probably only had moments to get this task accomplished and escape back out the tunnel before the security team got themselves organized and came back down.

She glanced over at Sam and saw that a menu had come up on the screen, its choices bewilderingly technical. He knew what he was doing, moving through the program with relative ease, apparently searching for something very specific. He brought up page after page of financial transactions.

"How are you doing?" Ally asked him.

"I think I've got it," he said. "Getting ready to print."

He'd barely finished the words, and Ally felt something cold press against the base of her skull. A woman's voice whispered, "Don't move or I'll put a bullet through your brain."

Angelic? Ally thought she recognized the voice, but there was no way to warn Sam. He was engrossed in the printer instructions. It didn't surprise Ally that Angelic was in on the criminal activities with Jason. Still, she'd never considered the woman capable of murder. Ally racked her brain, but couldn't come up with a way to disarm her without taking a terrible risk—and endangering Sam, if he tried to intervene.

Angelic nudged Ally forward into Sam's line of peripheral vision.

"Don't do anything stupid, Sinclair!" she ordered. "I have a gun on your girlfriend."

Sam whirled in the chair, his hands on the arms stopping cold when he saw what he was dealing with. Ally hadn't known whether to take Angelic seriously. Sam's expression told her the woman must look as crazy as she sounded.

"Abort the program," Angelic ordered. "Abort it now! Unless you want her brains splattered all over you!"

"Angelic—" Sam's voice was calm and reasonable "—you don't want to do that. Let's talk about this."

Angelic hissed like a she-cat. "Do it, Sinclair!" She dug the gun barrel into Ally's neck and released the safety.

Sam nodded. He turned and tapped out the commands

to close the program. Ally knew he would never risk her safely. Their only chance was for Ally to find some way to distract Angelic.

At the sound of another explosive click, Sam's fingers stilled on the keyboard. A bullet had been chambered, but it wasn't Angelic's gun.

"Jason?" Angelic said in a startled voice. "Thank God!"

Ally tilted her head just enough to see Jason Aragon holding a menacing Glock revolver in both hands, primed to shoot. He glared at Sam and Ally, as if deciding which one to target. Without warning, he swung on Angelic.

"Drop the gun," he told her.

"No!"

"Drop it! The safety didn't release. It won't fire."

Ally heard the terrifying rasp of metal hitting metal. Angelic had pulled the trigger but the gun hadn't fired. Ally's legs buckled beneath her, and only sheer determination kept her off the floor. She could have been dead, her brains splattered all over Sam.

Dazed, she watched Sam tackle Angelic and take her down with a bone-crushing thud. He easily wrestled the gun out of her hand and sent it spinning across the floor to Ally, who picked it up, but had no clue what to do with it. Possibly she should hold it on Angelic, as Jason was doing. Possibly she should hold it on Jason.

But neither seemed necessary. Sam had already pulled off his belt and bound Angelic's hands. Now he was using his bow tie as a gag. Ally glanced at the silent closet, aware that the man inside had stopped kicking. She wondered if he'd blacked out from shock. She almost had.

Finished with Angelic, Sam sprang up and took the

gun from Ally's hand. He tucked her in his arms, as if to shield her.

"What the hell are you doing?" he asked Aragon.

Jason had shoved his gun in a shoulder holster beneath his coat. He pulled out a badge. "I'm taking Angelic Dupree into custody. She and her partner, Abel Belen, created dummy holding companies to transfer large sums of money to offshore banks."

Sam was clearly confused. "That looks like a Treasury badge. What are you doing with it?"

Ally was more than confused. The man who'd held her hostage was a federal agent? That was almost beyond her comprehension.

Sam hesitated, and Ally wondered if Sam was going to reveal that he worked for the department, too. Instead he said, "If you're an agent, why haven't you arrested Angelic before this?"

"I'd planned to," Jason explained. "We were getting ready to shut down the entire operation, and then you showed up. So I held off, thinking I might catch you in the net, too. My sources are now telling me that you're not and never were a corporate raider. They're telling me that you and I have something in common, Sam."

Jason smiled. "We *both* work undercover for the department."

Sam's laughter was cold. "They did a much better job of covering your ass than mine. None of my contacts there know anything about your undercover work."

"That's because I'm not officially an agent. Years ago the department gave me a choice—work for them or go to jail. They'd discovered the club was mired in corruption—and had been before I took it over from the family members who inherited it—and they would have prosecuted me if I hadn't agreed to cooperate. So, I became a crook to catch the crooks."

Ally felt compelled to ask whether that was when she was with him. But he was already looking at her, as if he'd read her mind.

"I don't expect you to believe me," he told her, "but I was actually trying to protect you and keep you away from the predators. If I seemed rough and overbearing, I apologize. I had to prove I was one of them, a tough guy."

Ally wasn't certain she didn't believe him. He looked almost contrite.

Sam clearly wasn't convinced. "You've been undercover for how many years? Why haven't they shut the operation down before?"

"I was recruited the same year I met Ally. And the operation wasn't shut down because the club was too good a lure. It gave the department access to the financial dealings of international business titans, and that's valuable in many ways."

He looked almost proud of himself as he added, "Don't think arrests haven't been made since I started feeding the department information. Some big timber had fallen, but the powers that be have found ways to keep the club out of it."

He glanced down at the woman sitting on the floor. "Angelic unknowingly brought in the cream, and the department skimmed it off the top. Very patiently, of course. Never more than one titan a year, along with his co-conspirators."

Sam seemed impressed, despite his obvious distaste for Jason's methods. "Now it's clear why the department was never able to infiltrate your operation," he said. "They already had infiltrated it."

"Yes, although as I said, I'm not officially an agent."

"Well, that's something else we have in common," Sam said. "I'm not officially on a case. I'm here for you, Jason. My name is Sam Wolverton. Ring a bell?"

"I know who you are, Sam."

Jason's voice had gone soft, and Ally was instantly nervous. She was in between two powerhouse men, both dangerous and capable of anything. She gave Sam's tux jacket a tug, hoping to defuse the tension, but he was fixed on his nemesis, and he was on the attack.

"Then you also know that this property belonged to my family before your family stole it and killed my great-grandfather? The ghosts haunting this house are my ancestors, Aragon. They're Wolvertons."

Jason didn't back off, either. "I know your great-grandfather was a drinker and a gambler. He lost this place to Jake Colby, and he ended up in jail for trying to kill Colby."

Sam's body tensed. Ally had her arm around him, and she could feel his spine go stiff.

"Micha Wolverton never drank a drop until after his wife took her life," Sam said. "He was a broken man, thanks to Colby, who's a distant relative of yours, Aragon. It was Colby who took Micha's business and his home—and drove his wife to suicide."

Even Angelic had stopped struggling against her bonds and was listening. Aware that both men were armed, Ally knew she had to do something.

She freed herself from Sam's hold. "It was a hundred years ago," she reminded both of them. "We'll never know what really happened—and it wouldn't resolve your differences if we did know."

Jason shrugged. "That's true. We'll never know what happened, but at the end of the day, it doesn't matter. The house and grounds are yours, Sam. The Willows belongs to the Wolvertons. It always has."

"What do you mean?" Sam asked.

An expectant silence filled the room.

"I couldn't take on this case without investigating my own family," Jason explained. "I had a title search done on this estate. What we found forced us to dig deeper. As it turns out, the title was transferred when your great-grandfather was in prison, and his name was forged. The house and grounds were never legally owned by the Colbys."

"And you've known this how long?"

Jason smiled. "A while. There was no way I—or anyone—could reveal the truth until this case was resolved. It is now, so, congratulations. You may not have a job when the department finds out about your rogue operation to bring me to justice, but you have a great house."

Sam's shoulders rose and fell. Tension released in a gust of air. Ally went to his side, glad to have an opportunity to support him for once. But as she slipped her arm through his, she saw someone hovering in the doorway behind Jason.

The tall, imposing man hesitated, gazing into the room for a moment. As he turned and left, Ally noticed that he wore a black waistcoat and tie that was wrapped outside his shirt collar and looped like a bow at his throat. No one else seemed to have noticed him, but Ally had already figured out who he was. She remembered his picture from among the photographs in the local history book.

While Sam and Jason had been resolving the ownership of The Willows, Ally may have just seen the real owner. Micha Wolverton was a tall, dark and strikingly handsome ghost, even after enduring a century in a graveyard. Ally knew she ought to be seriously questioning her sanity, but he had looked pleased at what he'd seen, and she was happy for him. Maybe there would be laughter in this house now instead of weeping.

# *Epilogue*

*Washington, D.C.*
*Two months later*

"ALLY, WHAT ARE you doing here, working on a Saturday?"

Ally looked up from the stack of papers she was sorting and gave her little sister a pained smile. "What are *you* doing here? Aren't you missing the replays of *Friday Night Smackdown?*"

Victoria, as Ally was now on orders to call her, shrugged and grinned. "Okay, so Mike's a little heavy into pro wrestling. It's his *only* flaw."

She batted her eyelashes, apparently as a testament to Mike's near perfection. "I need to borrow your brown sugar lipstick. Mike and I are celebrating our four-month anniversary of the day we realized we both love M. Night Shyamalan movies. We're going out for Indian food. Want to come?"

"Thanks, no. I'll celebrate by having the television remote all to myself. I'll probably get so dizzy flipping channels I'll fall off the couch. The lipstick is in my purse—the black mesh makeup bag."

Vix leaped upon her purse, which Ally had tossed on her catchall table with the coffeemaker, the air purifier and the hot rollers. As Vix searched through the contents, she spotted a foil-wrapped packet and held it up.

"A condom, Ally? What's that for?"

"Sticky fingers."

"What?"

"It's a Wet Wipe, Victoria." Ally kept sorting her papers—and did her best to ignore her sister. Vix had agreed to give her relationship with Mike some time before doing anything drastic, like getting married, and in the meantime, she'd moved back into Ally's Georgetown apartment. Mike might as well have moved in, too, for all the time he was spending there. It really was less crowded here in Ally's office on the weekends—and quieter.

When Ally looked up to see if her purse had survived, Vix was waggling the lipstick tube and observing Ally closely. Never a good thing.

"You didn't answer my question," she said in a sing-song voice.

"Which question was that?"

"Why are you here instead of somewhere else, where you could be having fun. Remember that word? Starts with an *F,* like every other *fun* word."

"Victoria, don't be crude. I have to get this place organized. It's a mess." She didn't bother to mention that her promotion to director of development had been a mixed blessing. Very mixed. She had no assistant, no budget, and already, the powers that be were talking about downsizing. How did you downsize from one employee?

"You organized it *last* weekend, and the weekend before that," Vix pointed out. "You need to get your life organized. That's the mess."

Ally wheeled her chair around to the row of file

cabinets behind her. She bent and opened one of the lowest drawers, intending to file copies of the correspondence that had been piling up. That's how desperate she was to look busy.

"Hello?" Vix suddenly appeared, kneeling and waving a hand in Ally's face. "You keep talking about going back to New Orleans to see Sam. How long has it been since you've had contact with him?"

Ally searched for the right file folder. "We…e-mail occasionally." Actually his last e-mail had been over a week ago, and all he'd done was ask how life was treating her. Sam always had been a man of few words, but that was ridiculous. It had been so brief and polite she hadn't even answered yet. She'd been too disappointed.

"E-mail? Ugh. You're avoiding him."

Ally sighed. "Or he's avoiding me. Did that ever occur to you?"

"No."

"No?" Ally looked around at her sister, who was shaking her head.

"Not a chance," Vix said. "The man's hooked. I was there. I saw the lust burning in his eyes when he looked at you. He was *burning* for you, Ally."

Ally's heart began to stir from its two-month slumber. "Really? Burning?"

"Yeah! Like on fire, like smoldering embers, like red-hot coals, like—" She grinned. "I could go on, but I'm starting to sweat."

"It *was* pretty hot for a while there," Ally had to admit. So hot that she'd felt awkward around Sam afterward. She really hadn't known quite what to say to him. Everything between them had been so quick and combustible, like a torch igniting.

There *she* went with the fire metaphors…but maybe he'd felt the same way.

"I honestly don't know what happened," she told Vix. "Sometimes I wonder if our mission to rescue you was the glue that held us together, and when it was over, we really knew very little about each other. And he didn't exactly beg me to stick around."

Ally had explained to him that she had obligations and had to go back to D.C., but she hadn't necessarily meant forever. She'd even dropped hints about how much she loved New Orleans, but he hadn't seemed to pick up on them, and finally she'd decided it was intentional. He didn't want her to stick around.

"You never should have left New Orleans," Vix said passionately. "You should have stayed there with him."

Ally stared at her sister in disbelief. "I had to come back here with you, didn't I? You were making big decisions. You needed someone to talk to, some stability."

"Ally, I have Mike to talk to. The decisions are his and mine."

"Yes, but a sounding board. A girl always needs a sounding board, and that's what big sisters are for."

"That's what cell phones are for. No matter where you are, you're just a cell phone call away."

"For heaven's sake, Victoria. I have a life here. I can't just walk away from it."

"What life?"

"This life! My job and everything I've worked for up to now. Our parents. My friends. *You.*"

"Job? You're hiding behind this job. You're afraid to

take risks. Our parents? They live in London, and you see them maybe twice a year. Me? I have my own life now, with Mike. No offense, Ally, but we're fine, Mike and I. We don't need a chaperone."

The fax phone rang, startling both of them. Seconds later a fax shot into the tray. Vix got to it before Ally could even move. She grabbed the single sheet and held it behind her back, apparently determined to keep it from her sister until she'd made her point.

"Ally," she said beseechingly, "Mike and I were hoping you'd let us sublet the apartment. I got the job at Macy's, and with both of us working we can make the rent. Plus, it's already furnished, which makes it perfect."

So, now Ally was being kicked out of her own apartment? She sniffed. "How can you say I don't take risks? Look what I did to get you out of that den of iniquity that I *thought* you were in."

"That was the finest moment of your life." Vix gave her a thumbs-up. "And you have me to thank for it."

No, Ally had Sam to thank. He was the one who'd made it possible for her to take those crazy risks. Not that she wouldn't have done it on her own, but with a man like Sam as her backup, all things had seemed possible. Funny how that felt like another life, another woman.

"Aren't you going to congratulate me on the job?" Vix said. "I start tomorrow, the sportswear department. They're training me to be a buyer."

"That's wonderful," Ally said, and meant it. "You've always had a flair for fashion. You'll be great."

She set the filing down. There was no way to concentrate with her sister on a mission. "Let's see that fax."

It was an estate sale notice, Ally realized as she took

the single sheet from Vix. She assumed it had come to the wrong office since she didn't deal with estate sales.

"Wait, what is this?" Ally's voice went faint as she read the fax more closely. The paper rattled in her hands. Vix popped around the desk for a look.

"The Willows?" Vix took the fax from Ally. "Isn't that Sam's house? Why is he having an estate sale? It says he's selling off everything. The house will probably be next."

Ally was too shocked to respond. Was he selling The Willows? Why would he do that when he'd worked so hard to get the house back? In one of his e-mails he'd told her about a trunk filled with family heirlooms that had been unearthed by the explosion he'd set in the tunnel. Inside he'd also found old stock certificates of Micha's that were worth millions so this sale couldn't be about money.

She read the notice again, wondering who'd sent it to her. Could it have been Sam, himself?

Ally had moved back to her own motel the day after Angelic was arrested. It was too awkward in Sam's suite with Vix and Mike there. That was when she'd let Sam know that she would be on her way back to Georgetown soon. Vix needed her big sister, and Ally had to return to work.

Sam had taken her out to dinner that evening. He'd told her the club had already been shut down and the computer system confiscated as evidence. He also shared that he hadn't lost his job. He'd just extended his personal leave to make some decisions about the house—and his life. But he'd been so quiet about everything else that Ally had decided she should get out of his way, and not clutter his thoughts with things he wasn't ready to deal with.

She'd talked about New Orleans, but she'd never said a word about them, their relationship. What relationship?

Sam was a quiet man. And she had clearly made a mistake when she'd told him she loved him. Or that she wanted to tell him she loved him. Or whatever it was she'd said. That was when things had started going wrong. Probably. She wasn't sure. You could never be sure of anything with quiet people, and Ally wasn't good with ambiguity.

She couldn't tell her little sister any of this, though. Vix wasn't quiet, and she would never stop harping about what a wimp Ally was.

"Ally, are you listening?"

"Sure, Vix, sure."

"That's *Victoria,* Ally. Why is it so hard to remember that your sister's name is Victoria?"

Vix droned on about how Ally had never really cared about what was important to her and had never allowed her to take the initiative and be her own person. She was really on a tear, but Ally wasn't listening anymore. She read the fax again, her mind starting to whir with ideas.

"Maybe," Ally murmured.

"Maybe what?" Vix said.

Ally didn't answer. She was caught up with the possibilities. Maybe Vix was right about this life stuff. Maybe this was the day Ally would start living life for herself, rather than for her parents, her sister, her job, all of which she loved—and all of which could take care of themselves.

Maybe this *was* that day.

"Hello?" Ally knocked on the carved double doors, which were hanging open a crack. No one answered, but that didn't surprise her. The house already looked as if it were falling into disarray. The grass needed mowing and the hedges needed trimming. Uncollected mail had piled up in the front portico, and of course, there were no lovely security guards in the anteroom.

But it was still a beautiful place, regal and elegant.

It was still The Willows.

She let herself in, aware first of the feathery dust that coated even the vast expanse of hardwood floor. As she stepped into the foyer, the dust rippled like a veil. It could have been an endless bridal train of dove-gray velvet. The chandeliers were soft and muted, too, their crystal facets rounded and glowing like pearls in the waning sunlight.

Strange and magical, Ally thought. The place was even more haunting in its emptiness. You could almost hear the echoes of the past. And there was a sadness hanging in the air, too. She wondered if anyone was ever happy here, if the halls ever rang with laughter.

"Hello?" she called again, aware of the futility of being heard by someone in another part of the huge house. She had no idea if Sam were even here. She hadn't called before coming. The trip had been an impulse, and something as simple as disinterest in his tone could have killed it. She couldn't risk speaking with him first. She had to come here and deal with him in person.

As she approached the stairway to the second floor, she heard a faint sound. *Hoo hoo hoo.* It seemed to be coming from the east wing, the one that was never used. Soft more than distant, it reminded her of a mourning dove's call.

She headed off toward the east-wing, compelled by the eerily familiar sound. Her heart hesitated as she spotted the stairway to the upper floor. She'd never been in this wing, even when she'd stayed here with Jason. As she rushed up the stairs and down the hallway, she heard the sound again.

It wasn't a dove's cry, she realized. It was a woman's. Somewhere nearby, she was weeping. A heartrending sound, and Ally thought she heard it coming from the double doors at the end of the hallway. That must be the master bedroom.

Fear gripped her as she opened the doors and saw Sam standing at one of the bedroom's Palladian windows. He looked out at the graveyard, and right next to him, gazing out also, was a woman in a long white gown. It could have been the gown Ally wore when she was masquerading as The White Rose.

"Sam?" Ally could barely hear herself speak, but Sam caught it. As he turned, he looked right through the woman, who faded to an outline before she vanished entirely.

"Ally, what are you doing here?"

"Sam, did you see her?"

"Who?"

"The woman looking out the window. She was standing right next to you." She hurried over to him. "I know this sounds crazy, but I think it was Rose. I've seen her before, in the lower level. She led me to the passageway—and she was just here, in this room."

Ally pointed to the portrait of Rose on the fireplace mantle. Sam himself had described it to Ally, but right now, he was looking at her as if she *were* crazy.

Ally sighed. Maybe she was. "Okay, never mind," she said.

"What brings you here?" he asked her. "Are you in town on business?"

She could hardly keep the exasperation out of her voice. "Sam, you sent me a fax about your estate sale. Why would you even consider selling this place?"

"I didn't send you a fax. Ally? Are you all right?"

"Who sent it then? *Are* you selling this place?" She sounded like a woman betrayed. She could hear the emotion in her voice, but that was ridiculous. This wasn't her house. It was his. He could do anything he wanted with it.

"It looks that way, yes," he said.

*"Why?"*

"Why? What am I going to do with it? Rattle around here all by myself? It's huge. It's a mausoleum."

"How can you say that, Sam? It's beautiful. This place deserves a chance to be happy again."

"The *house* deserves happiness? Are you serious?"

"Yes, actually, I am serious." He didn't seem to get it, and that upset her even more. If she could feel the rich legacy of this place, and the promise for it to be something extraordinary now that it had been restored to its rightful owners, why couldn't he, a Wolverton? These were his ancestors hanging around for an entire century, waiting for him to do the right thing and make this place a home.

"Ally, are you here because of the house?"

She was sorely tempted to say yes. She'd been on the brink of making of a fool of herself since she walked in the door, and she needed a safe out. But she hadn't come all the way from Washington, D.C., to play games. They'd already done plenty of that.

"I came to explain to you why I left. You must have been wondering about that, right?" *You were wondering, weren't you? You'd better have been.*

"You had to go. Your sister, your job, that's what you said."

God, men were so literal. "I left because I thought Victoria needed me more than you did, Sam. You never said anything. You never *did* anything."

"Yeah, I know." His head came up, and he looked at her searchingly, at her eyes and her mouth and her expression, as if he was trying to read her mind.

"You know?" She was not getting the right answers from this man. And where was the burning lust that Vix had mentioned? Even a damn spark would help.

He scratched his neck. He sighed. He shook his head. "I had some things to get figured out. I needed some time."

Something flared like fire through her chest. It was the breath she'd just taken. Was he saying exactly what she feared? That he didn't want a relationship, or at least not one with her? Wasn't that the way all men did it? They said they wanted time, space?

Her voice went icy cold. "And did you get those things figured out, Sam?"

He seemed to have withdrawn, gone into his reflective mode. "It's not in me to be with another vulnerable, desperate woman. I've done that. People get hurt. Badly."

"I'm not vulnerable, and I'm certainly not desperate."

"And there's my job, Ally. It doesn't allow for a relationship."

"That is *such* a load of crap, Sam. This has nothing to do with your job. Why don't you just tell the truth and save us both some time?"

His golden eyebrows furrowed. "I am telling the truth."

"Then why did you look to the left? You taught me how to read a lie, mister, and I just read one."

"Jesus," he whispered, raking a hand through his hair, "I'm trying to tell you that I don't have a good track record with relationships. I think I'm cursed, Ally. I think the whole damn family is cursed and always has been. The Wolvertons are doomed to destroy each other."

"Cursed? Doomed?" Her voice went raspy, and she couldn't bear to have him see how upset she was. Heartbroken. Her heart was breaking, dammit. "I guess that's plain enough, isn't it."

She wheeled around and headed for the door, muttering, "This will teach me to call first." But before she could get there, the door slammed shut and the dead bolt turned, right before her eyes.

She felt a cold draft around her ankles, and the air was suddenly thick and fragrant. Roses. She smelled roses. "Sam, what's going on?"

"I don't know." He came over and tried the dead bolt. It wouldn't turn over, even when he applied some muscle. And Sam had muscle.

"We're locked in," he said.

She looked at him and saw her own disbelief mirrored in his expression. He had not set this up. He didn't know what was going on anymore than she did. "Did you hear that?" Someone was laughing out in the hallway. Laughing uproariously.

"It's her," Ally said. "It's the White Rose."

Sam cocked his head, listening. "Sounds like a man to me."

"It's both of them. They locked us in here."

"Ally, do you actually believe in ghosts?"

"*Sam,* can't you smell the roses?"

"I thought that was you."

The laughter had grown distant, but Ally suddenly understood. "They're matchmaking, Sam. They want us together."

Her heart literally rocketed into her throat as she looked up at him.

His face was the same crazy kaleidoscope of emotions she remembered from when she'd declared her feelings in the balcony room. For a moment, she thought he might vanish into thin air, just like his ancestors. Instead he shook his head and mumbled something.

"What did you say?"

He turned away and whipped back, almost angry. "I said they're smart ghosts. *I* want us together, too. I've always wanted that."

"You've *always* wanted that? Then why didn't you tell me?"

He sighed deeply. "Men are stupid."

"They *are*." She wanted to laugh, but as she gazed up at him she saw something change in his eyes. "What is it?" she asked.

"Speaking of holding things back, why the hell didn't you tell *me* that you were a princess?"

"You—you did a background check on me?"

"Background, foreground, high ground, low ground. I know the exact moment of your birth, Allegra Danner, the name of the doctor who took out your royal tonsils—and your bra size."

"Really? My tonsils? That's pretty private stuff."

His voice went husky. "And you thought I didn't need you."

Dear God. She could hardly speak he thrilled her so. "Sometimes women are stupid, too."

"Maybe everybody's stupid when it comes to love."

Ally wasn't quite so sure about that. From her recent experience, there was a wisdom to love that surpassed every other kind. It was pure and real and searingly intense. It cut to the bone, and people got hurt, just as Sam had said, which was why the intellect distrusted the emotion and tried to suppress it. When love got dangerously intense, the intellect took over, reasoning the feelings away to protect the lover from rejection and heartbreak.

Hell, she and Sam had been on the brink of both the entire time.

But now, as he brushed her lips with his thumb, she could feel the tenderness, the nakedness in his touch. He was open, honest.

Miserable maybe, but honest.

"Okay," he said.

"Okay what?"

"It's good. It's all good. Ghosts, curses, doom, whatever."

She found herself wanting to laugh with joy, and she wondered if somewhere in the house, Micha and Rose were laughing still.

"I don't want to sell this place, Ally, but I don't want to be here without you, either. It's empty without you. It's sad."

She fell into his arms, and he picked her up off the ground with a deep, aching groan. "I don't like this vulnerability stuff," he said. "It's insane. It shouldn't be happening to a guy like me."

"Vulnerability is good, Sam."

"Next you're going to say desperation is good, too."

"It *is*. Desperate love? There's nothing sweeter. You

don't think Rose and Micha were desperate all these years? You don't think that's what all the howling and weeping was about?"

"I thought that was me howling and weeping. God, I've missed you and your asthmatic kitten snores."

She stared him straight in the eyes, and all the need in her hungry soul, all of the longing in her patiently waiting heart, flooded out of her. But with it came a rush of doubts and questions. "What about your job? My job, for that matter."

"I'm on personal leave, indefinitely. What about you?"

"My budget's been cut. They'd probably be thrilled if I took some time. One less salary to pay."

"See? We have plenty of time to get the logistics figured out." He glanced at the doorway. "I don't think they're letting us out of here for a while anyway."

"What if they never let us out? Maybe— Do you think there could be a passageway in the fireplace?" Curious, she turned and started toward the fireplace. The tug on her hand whipped her around and into his arms like a tango dancer.

"That isn't the passageway I'm interested in," Sam said, his voice rough with rising passion.

Rising being the operative word, Ally realized as he dropped his hands to her fanny and possessively gathered her close. The sweetest of thrills shot through her. Apparently, he *had* missed her. His eyes were burning like fire. Vix would be pleased.

"So, you think you know all my secrets?" she challenged.

"Oh, no, I have lots of exploring to do. Of you and the house."

He bent to her, hovering just at her lips. "I love you," he said.

The house seemed to sigh with relief. And the heady perfume of roses swirled through the rooms.

"Well, it's no secret that I love you, too."

She laughed and soft sounds of mirth rose to join hers. Suddenly she and Sam were surrounded by happy sighs and murmurs of approval.

"Privacy could be a problem," she said in a wry tone.

"I'm sure they'll find ways to keep busy." He was clearly interested in her and her alone at the moment.

"So, now you believe in ghosts?"

"I believe in you and me."

Ally tilted her head back to accept his kiss and the warmth of it gushed all through her, part healing balm, part fiery natural aphrodisiac. She was in a strange old house with a man who was terrified of vulnerability and had hang-ups with relationships, but this was right. It was real. After years of feeling like a displaced person, she was home. Sam was home. *Everyone* was home.

\* \* \* \* \*

New York Times *bestselling author*
*Linda Lael Miller*
*is back with a new romance featuring*
*the heartwarming McKettrick family*
*from Silhouette Special Edition.*

*SIERRA'S HOMECOMING*
*by Linda Lael Miller*

*On sale December 2006,*
*wherever books are sold.*

*Turn the page for a sneak preview!*

Soft, smoky music poured into the room.

The next thing she knew, Sierra was in Travis's arms, close against that chest she'd admired earlier, and they were slow dancing.

Why didn't she pull away?

"Relax," he said. His breath was warm in her hair.

She giggled, more nervous than amused. What was the matter with her? She was attracted to Travis, had been from the first, and he was clearly attracted to her. They were both adults. Why not enjoy a little slow dancing in a ranch-house kitchen?

Because slow dancing led to other things. She took a step back and felt the counter flush against her lower back. Travis naturally came with her, since they were holding hands and he had one arm around her waist.

Simple physics.

Then he kissed her.

Physics again—this time, not so simple.

"Yikes," she said, when their mouths parted.

He grinned. "Nobody's ever said that after I kissed them."

She felt the heat and substance of his body pressed against hers. "It's going to happen, isn't it?" she heard herself whisper.

"Yep," Travis answered.

"But not tonight," Sierra said on a sigh.

"Probably not," Travis agreed.

"When, then?"

He chuckled, gave her a slow, nibbling kiss. "Tomorrow morning," he said. "After you drop Liam off at school."

"Isn't that…a little…soon?"

"Not soon enough," Travis answered, his voice husky. "Not nearly soon enough."

# nocturne™

**Explore the dark and sensual
new realm of paranormal romance.**

# HAUNTED
### BY LISA CHILDS

**The first book in the riveting
new 3-book miniseries, Witch Hunt.**

# DEATH CALLS
### BY CARIDAD PIÑEIRO

**Darkness calls to humans,
as well as vampires…**

*On sale December 2006,
wherever books are sold.*

# REQUEST YOUR FREE BOOKS!

## 2 FREE NOVELS
## PLUS 2
## FREE GIFTS!

HARLEQUIN®

*Blaze*

**Red-hot reads!**

HB06

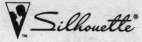

# HARLEQUIN®

## Blaze™

# COMING NEXT MONTH

### #291 THE MIGHTY QUINNS: DECLAN Kate Hoffmann
*The Mighty Quinns, Bk. 3*
Security expert Declan Quinn isn't exactly thrilled with his latest job, acting as bodyguard for radio sex-pert Rachel Merrell—until she drags him into her bed and shows him what *other* things he can do to her body while he's guarding it....

### #292 SECRET SANTA Janelle Denison, Isabel Sharpe, Jennifer LaBrecque
*(A Naughty but Nice Christmas Collection)*
*Christmas.* Whether it's spending sensual nights cuddled up by the fire or experiencing the thrill of being caught under the mistletoe by a secret admirer, *anything* is possible at this time of year. Especially when Santa himself is delivering sexy little secrets....

### #293 IT'S A WONDERFULLY SEXY LIFE Hope Tarr
*Extreme*
Baltimore street cop Mandy Delinski doesn't believe in lust at first sight—at least until she's almost seduced by gorgeous Josh Thornton at a Christmas party. Talk about a holiday miracle! For once it looks as if she's going to get *exactly* what she wants for Christmas—until she finds her "perfect gift" in the morgue the next day....

### #294 WITH HIS TOUCH Dawn Atkins
*Doing It...Better!*
With no notice, Sugar Thompson's business partner Gage Maguire started a seduction campaign...on *her.* That's against all the rules they established years ago. Sure, he's tempting her. Only, it's too bad he seems to want more than the temporary fling she has in mind....

### #295 BAD INFLUENCE Kristin Hardy
*Sex & the Supper Club II, Bk. 1*
Paige Favreau has always taken the safe path. Career, friends, lovers—she's enjoyed them all, but none have rocked her world. Until blues guitarist Zach Reed challenges her to take a walk on the wild side....

### #296 A TASTE OF TEMPTATION Carrie Alexander
*Lust Potion #9, Bk. 3*
After a mysterious lust potion works its sexy magic on her pals, gossip columnist Zoe Aberdeen wants to know the story behind it. When she asks her neighbor—and crime lab scientist—Donovan Shane for help, he's not interested. But thanks to Zoe's "persuasive" personality, he's soon testing the potion and acting out his every fantasy with the sassy redhead....

HBCNM1106